CRYPTID KILLERS

ALISTER HODGE

SEVERED PRESS
HOBART TASMANIA

CRYPTID KILLERS

WWW.SEVEREDPRESS.COM

ISBN: 978-1-922551-95-5

CHAPTER ONE

Icy wind tore at Dave's clothes, rocking his body where he crouched on the ski slope. A frown creased his forehead as he examined the wallaby carcass. Blood spattered the snow about the creature, or what was left of it. Only the upper half remained. Pink, flaccid lungs hung from the base of its torso, a violent contrast to the sleek fur of its neck.

Wild dogs?

No. This far into winter they'd have retreated below the snow line. He pulled off a glove and touched the body. It was cold, but the meat had yet to freeze. Whatever had killed the animal was likely still close. He sat back on his heels for a moment, searching the alpine bush. Snow whipped past his ankles in a white haze, the wind howling a funeral dirge of emptiness. Giving up, he sighed and looked back at the wallaby. Anything with a sense for survival had fled these slopes long before, seeking shelter from the coming storm.

Dave dragged the corpse into a stand of snow gum before covering the bloodied section of ski run with fresh snow. Leaving it in the open would only invite a barrage of complaints from the resort's guests.

God forbid any unpleasantness disturb their precious holiday.

His lip curled at the thought. Selfish, rich bastards that could barely wipe their own arse; the only sort who could afford the alpine resort for which he worked. Well, at least he didn't work front of house. How the wait staff and concierge kept their cool dealing with people like that all day, he'd never know.

The afternoon was getting late. With the sun hidden by clouds, the frigid air had become bone-shatteringly cold. This high up in the Australian Alps, the weather could change at the drop of a hat. He shoved the next marker flag deep into the powdery snow, then stood and stretched his back. Dave made sure his co-worker was out of sight, before extracting a battered hip flask from an inner pocket of his jacket. Despite wearing thick gloves, he unscrewed the top with ease and took a swig of whiskey. Everything ached after the past two weeks of preparations for the coming race. The one-hundred kilometre Alpine Enduro event would become the longest cross-country ski race in Australia, and headline a festival to launch Silver-Trust's luxury ski resort. Hearing the crunch of approaching feet in the snow, he quickly stowed the flask and turned.

"That's the last of the markers, Trish."

Her eyes flicked to the pocket holding his flask and back to his face, lips narrowing slightly. For a moment, he thought she'd lecture him for drinking on the job again, instead, she looked down the valley. Clouds had already blocked the view of the resort, climbing the mountain slopes in a roiling mass of white and grey.

"We need to clear out before the storm hits."

Trish walked away, boots leaving deep holes in the powder as she cut across the slope to their 4WD Landcruiser. Glaring at her receding back, Dave pulled out his flask again and drained the remaining whiskey in two swallows. The woman had started working for Silver-Trust long after him, and yet she'd been made his supervisor.

What a fucking joke.

As Dave shouldered the last of their work gear to follow in Trish's footsteps, the first snow of the coming storm whipped past, a spattering of flakes catching in his beard. By the time he dumped his tools in the back of the Landcruiser, gale-force winds rocked the vehicle. He climbed inside and slammed the door.

"Took your bloody time," muttered Trish, turning the key in the ignition.

As the engine roared to life, Dave stared over his shoulder out the back window. The vista of gumtrees and ski trails had been obliterated by a white chaos of wind and snow, visibility reduced to metres. Trish put the car into reverse and spun the wheel, preparing to do a three-point-turn.

"What are you doing?" asked Dave. "We can't drive down the mountain in a storm like this. You'll wind up crashing off the trail."

Trish glared at him. "Well, it's not like *you* can drive us anywhere. How much whiskey did you get through, Dave? If you'd stuck to coffee, we'd have finished hours ago and be home by now."

Dave clenched his jaw. "Don't know what you're talking about. I haven't touched a drop since the last warning." The lie ran easily off his tongue. "But driving in a storm like this isn't safe. There's a supply hut for the race further up this track. If we're smart, we take cover until it blows over."

Dave wasn't fussed if he got stuck on the mountain overnight. He had a spare bottle of Johnny Walker in his swag, and a night away from the shit hole he called home wouldn't be a loss. Trish bit her bottom lip for a moment, then sighed and put the vehicle into first gear. The tyre chains bit into the snow and the car slowly pushed up the road.

Snow scooted past the windscreen as he searched for the hut marker, so thick Dave could barely see the trail's edge.

"There it is," he said, pointing out a yellow sign.

Trish eased to a stop, leaving the Landcruiser on the track. All work crews carried emergency gear. With the right shelter and clothing, a storm was little more than an inconvenience. Without them though, hypothermia and death were a certainty. Dave hauled two swags out of the back and walked toward the hut, leaning into the wind to keep his feet. Wind lashed the snow gums to either side, snapping dead wood and whipping branches into a frenzy.

Twenty paces off the fire-trail, a hut emerged from the storm. Constructed of grey metal sheeting, it hunkered low to the ground, standing little over head height above the snow drift. They had been there earlier in the day, stocking energy bars and water for the Enduro competitors. Dave shouldered open the door, accidently kicking a boot load of snow inside as he stumbled through the entrance.

Trish crowded in behind him and slammed the door shut again. After a search in the gloom, Dave found the light switch. A single bulb stuttered to life, its weak yellow light doing little to banish the darkness. Wind screamed outside, making the walls shudder under the force of each gust. Dave rubbed his hands together, his breath a plume of steam in the sickly light. There was no heating in the shed, but it would serve as a windbreak against the storm's ferocity. Shelving units stocked with food and water lined three walls, leaving enough space on the concrete floor for three adults to sleep shoulder to shoulder. Dave rolled out his swag and stuffed a sleeping bag inside.

Thinking of the whiskey bottle cradled in his pack, he stood and made for the door. "You need anything else from the Landcruiser while I'm there?"

Trish shook her head as she held up her phone for a signal. "Not unless there's a satellite dish I forgot about."

Dave pulled the hood of his jacket over his head, bracing himself to re-enter the storm. A gust caught the lip of the door, nearly ripping it from his grasp as he left the building. Outside, he paused for a moment, getting his bearings to the truck.

Something red caught his eye.

A slaughtered wallaby, exactly the same as the one he'd moved off the ski run, lay outside the hut. Hair prickled up the back of Dave's neck, a strange sensation that he was being watched causing him to look up.

"Anyone out there?" he yelled. He might as well have whispered. The force of the gale overpowered his words, whipping them into the storm. Flying sleet and snow reduced his world to no more than ten paces in any direction. Dave took a step back towards the hut, his need for a drink suddenly not quite as pressing. But then an eddy in the wind provided a glimpse of the SUV, not thirty paces away.

Don't be such an old wimp. Few glasses of Johnny and you'll be all good.

Dave leaned into the wind and marched for the Landcruiser, determined to be outside for the shortest possible time. As he reached the back of the vehicle, a metallic chirp cut through the storm's rage. It was a sound he felt in his chest as much as heard, like a cicada on steroids. Dave fumbled the key in the car's door, his eyes searching for the origin of the noise. The chirp sounded again, and this time he spied an almost human-like shape in the trees. Dave did a double-take, but when he glanced back again, it was gone.

You're losing it, old man.

He pulled his pack free and hooked a strap over one shoulder. A gust of wind ripped his hood back, and with his thick ski gloves, he struggled to pull it back over his head. The chirp sounded again, this time louder, punching into his chest like he was standing next to a concert speaker. The noise was unnatural, didn't belong in the winter landscape of a national park. Dave's eyes were wide, skin pale as he looked behind him, searching the swirling snow in each direction. Suddenly his foot was ripped from beneath him, smashing his shin into the base of the vehicle.

Something was beneath the car.

Another vicious tug, and he was on his back in the snow, arms flailing. A strangled yelp left his mouth as fangs ripped into the flesh above his boot. Dave kicked blindly with his other foot, his heel crunching into something hard. It did nothing to dissuade his attacker, teeth sliced deeper into his calf with every movement, tearing a scream of agony from Dave's lungs. If he didn't do something fast, it felt like his foot would be ripped clean off. In desperation, he sat up and reached blindly under the vehicle, searching for an eye to gouge. Expecting the fur of a dog, his fingers instead slipped over something smooth and wet. The beast released his leg, and suddenly it had his hand instead, teeth worrying back and forth.

Dave wrenched backwards, and with a sickening crunch and sound of tearing fabric, he was free. He scooted backward, his right hand a burning mess, severed arteries squirting crimson to steam on the snow.

Chest tight and heart smashing at his ribs, Dave climbed to his feet and broke into an ungainly sprint for the safety of the shed. His injured ankle was shot, severed tendons and muscle stopping the joint from working properly. He stumbled, ankle giving way as the chirp sounded from behind again. Somehow, Dave kept his feet. The shed was less than ten paces away now, he was going to make it.

"Trish, open the door!"

Something punched into his lower back knocking him off balance. Dave slammed into the wall of the shed, nose mashing sideways against the metal panel. Unsteadily, he got to his feet, stars dancing before his eyes as the door opened.

"What the fuck, Dave? There's no need to be a dick," muttered Trish, forehead creased in anger as she opened the door. Her eyes widened, mouth dropping open as she caught sight of him. Dave limped through the opening, slammed the door shut and leaned against it, panting.

"Jesus, your fingers are missing. What happened?"

Dave looked down at his hand for the first time. Only the thumb remained, all four fingers and part of his palm severed in a crescent-shaped bite. Blood spattered onto the concrete, streaming from his ankle and hand alike.

He struggled to form words to answer, agony lanced his chest with every shallow breath. Dave coughed, bringing blood to his lips. He reached his good hand behind his back to where he'd been hit, and the fingers came away red. *Stabbed?* The metallic chirp sounded again, loud over the howling wind.

Dave staggered to one of the shelving units. "We need to barricade the door," he spluttered, the words wet in the back of his throat. The sentence brought on a fit of coughing, scarlet misting the air before his face.

"Stop it, Dave, you're scaring me." Trish shrank away from him, her face pale, pupils dilated.

"There's no time," he coughed. "Please, I can't do this on my own."

Something smashed into the door, buckling the panel inwards. The lock held, but only barely. Dave drove his shoulder into the shelf, ignoring the burning of his hand as the stump mashed against it. He was feeling light headed, vision starting to grey from blood loss and pain. The blow to the door broke Trish's indecision, and as she leant her strength, the heavy shelf finally slid across the floor.

But it was too late.

The beast crashed into the door again, and this time the lock burst from the door jamb. A maelstrom of wind and snow entered the room. Trish screamed as she backed away, Dave's breath catching in his throat as he stared at the beast in the doorway. His ankle gave way as he lurched back, the tendons finally tearing through. He hit the deck hard. Fresh agony pierced his chest as something tore inside the wound, blood flooding his lungs. He knew he wouldn't survive, also knew that he'd been a selfish bastard most of his life. But maybe he could atone for some of it.

The creature ducked through the doorway, eyes fixed on the old man. Dave met its gaze, dry swallowing.

"Trish, wait until it attacks me," he wheezed, blood gurgling with every word. "Then fucking run for it."

Crimson dripped from the beast's mouth, clawed hands gripping his shoulders as it leaned close.

"RUN!"

CHAPTER TWO

"Wake up, soldier boy. We'll be there shortly."

Carter's eyes blinked open. He stifled a yawn as he sat straighter in the passenger seat, stretching his neck to ease an aching muscle. Carter grimaced at the landscape outside his window. When last awake, they'd been driving through green countryside, and yet now, they were above the snow line. To either side of the road, snow gums reached for the sky, their branches laden with glistening snow in the afternoon sun. The road itself was largely clear, with only the occasional dusting of white where branches overhead provided shade.

"Shit, how long have I been asleep?"

"Couple of hours." His new colleague, Agent Sophia Rylan, gave him a sideways glance before fixing back on the road. "What name do you prefer me to use, first or last? Just don't expect me to use some bullshit army nickname."

"Aside from my parents, no-one's called me Eoin since I was a kid."

"What, not even your wife?"

"*Ex*-wife."

Rylan raised an eyebrow. "Okay, surname it is then."

Having met her for the first time earlier that day, Carter had yet to get a bearing on his new boss. Rylan's accent was difficult to pin down, her words a mongrel mix of British, American and Australian inflections. Her facial expressions were guarded, providing zero insight to her thoughts. He glanced sideways for a second. Age was hard to guess, but with little else to go on, the time and expertise required to attain Rylan's status within the organisation meant she must at least be in her forties.

However, if he was going on physical attributes, she had the lean athleticism and biomechanics of someone a decade younger.

Rylan took another sip from her travel mug before setting it back in the cup holder. "What do you make of the case notes?"

Carter opened the manilla folder on his lap. Printed at the top of each page was his new ASIO branch name, Cryptid Investigation Unit. He flicked to the back and took out the summary page, his eyes drawn to the words he'd underlined earlier; hibernation, hunger and feasting.

"Ah, to tell the truth, I'm still getting my head around what we do, let alone the rest of it," said Carter. The clerk who'd given him the folder had welcomed him as the new 'Cryptid Killer' in town.

Fresh out of the army, working as an Agent for the Australian Security Intelligence Organisation (ASIO) was a career pivot for Carter. During a decade of service in the Australian SAS, he'd survived several tours in Afghanistan until his truck had driven over an improvised explosive device. That bastard bit of luck had seen him medevaced to a hospital in Germany. The following months were a blur of operations, pain and rehab, until he'd been medically discharged from the army with a fucked hip joint and half a pound of shrapnel still lodged in various parts of his body. Carter knew he should consider himself lucky, the only other soldier to survive the explosion was missing a leg and shitting into a colostomy bag. But after all his sacrifices, being ditched like a defective weapon still pissed him off.

He'd figured ASIO would be an opportunity to use his unique knowledge set, and was pleased to make it through the tough recruitment process. As a new agent, Carter had expected to combat terrorist threats and espionage, not be attached to a secret team that investigated 'cryptids'.

"What even *is* a cryptid?" asked Carter, trying to keep his tone neutral.

"You got to be kidding me," muttered Rylan under her breath. "Did they really not give you a briefing?"

Carter shrugged. "I was told you'd fill in the gaps. Wouldn't be my first mission where the bosses kept their cards close."

"Fine. A cryptid's an animal whose existence is disputed or unproven."

Carter inwardly groaned. "So, we're hunting Bigfoot?"

Rylan clenched her jaw, keeping her eyes on the road. "The *Sasquatch* is an American cryptid, but seeing as we're in the Australian Alps, its equivalent would be a Yowie. Look, most of the stories out there are just that – good tales to tell about the campfire. But it's a big world. There are intelligent creatures who prefer to stay unnoticed until something drives them into the open. And when that happens, people tend to die. It's our job to prevent that from happening."

Rylan glanced at him. "Look, just keep an open mind."

"Why me?" Carter's irritation finally won through. "If this job's to investigate urban legends, or tramp through the bush looking for a Tasmanian tiger, what the hell do you want with an ex-soldier? Surely a zoologist or park ranger would be better suited."

Rylan barked a laugh. "You'd be surprised what this job comes across. It isn't all cute critters, my friend. But you're the third ex-soldier sent my way. I'm starting to think the military's keeping tabs on my work. Those bastards are always on the lookout for something to use as a weapon."

Carter grunted acknowledgement. He'd worked in the forces long enough to know her concerns were probably well founded. "I'm ex-army, remember? If that shit's happening, I've not been briefed. And besides, my chain of command is now within ASIO. They can't compel me to speak unless our bosses give it the okay."

"Good. I've no desire to see more biological weapons developed on my watch. As far as I'm concerned, we're here to ensure these beasts stick to the shadows and out of society's way."

"So why do they call us 'Cryptid Killers' back at base?" asked Carter.

Rylan frowned. "Once theses beasts come out of hiding, sometimes they refuse to go quietly. If they present a risk to human life, it's our job to put them down."

The penny finally dropped. "So that's where I come in," said Carter.

"Well, knowing which way to point a gun doesn't hurt."

Carter stared out his side window, the unplanned beauty of the national park replaced by landscaped symmetry as they entered the grounds of Silver-Trust Ski Lodge. Built over the preceding five years, fierce protests against its destruction of pristine, alpine forest had sporadically reached the news. Somewhat unsurprisingly, money had won the day. It had only taken a sizable donation to vaporise government opposition to the project. Three hundred million dollars gifted to the Federal Snowy Mountains pumped-hydro scheme, and suddenly every hurdle disappeared. Ancient Snow Gum forests had subsequently fallen beneath Silver-Trust's axe, cleared for ski-runs, chairlifts and five-star accommodation.

Backlit by the late afternoon sun, a multi-story behemoth sprawled across the valley floor. Out of place in the national park surrounding, the building would have been better suited to the Gold Coast foreshore. The place was heaving with people. Men and women in designer snow-wear congregated before a temporary outdoor stage, fawning over stars of the European ski world. Silver-Trust had exported the best international long distance cross-country skiers to help launch the resort. Although the ski runs climbing the mountain were empty, come tomorrow, they would open for the first time. Rylan drove past the crowd at a crawl, heading for the underground car park.

Carter looked down at the folder on his lap and picked up the summary once again. “There’s not a whole lot in the file. What’s drawn your interest?”

“A series of murders and disappearances stretching back over a century.” Rylan paused and rolled down her window for a security check. After a moment, the guard waved them onwards and they drove down a steep concrete ramp into the bowels of the hotel. “Since the late 1870s people have gone missing at intervals of thirty years, and I had this year marked as the next anniversary. Two days ago, I received notice of yet another unexplained killing.”

“You’re talking about a period of one hundred and fifty years,” said Carter. “It’s got to be a coincidence; nothing lives that long.”

“And this is where you need to start thinking outside the box. I’ve got some personal experience in this area. Trust me, some animals live for extraordinarily long times. Take the Greenland shark for example; they can live up to five hundred years, and don’t even hit sexual maturity until they hit the ripe old age of one hundred and fifty.”

"But…" Carter trailed off, biting his tongue. He'd seen some weird shit on deployment when scouting caves for Taliban. Things that to this day he couldn't explain logically. Maybe it was time for him to shut up and approach the mission with an open mind.

Rylan pulled into an empty car space and turned off the engine. "We might find nothing of interest. Unfortunately, much of what we do involves chasing down false leads," she said before meeting his gaze. Carter saw a glint of excitement in her eye. "But, when the pieces fall into place, and you come head to head with a creature that until that moment existed only in legend? That, my friend, makes all the other bullshit worthwhile."

Carter nodded, a half-smile hooking one corner of his mouth. Even if the job ended up being quiet most of the time, it had to be better than getting poked full of shrapnel in the Afghan dust.

"We'll check in, then start with an examination of the victims," said Rylan.

Carter climbed out of the car, his injured hip complaining at the lengthy period of immobility. Forcing himself not to limp, he walked to the boot and hauled their two packs free. After a quick look to ensure they were alone in the car park, he unlocked a hidden compartment in the boot's floor, lifted the lid and exposed a weapon's locker holding three rifles and a spare pistol with ammunition. Rylan and Carter already carried a Glock each, and with any luck, the rifles would stay in the safe untouched. Happy that all appeared in order, he locked up, and followed his colleague to the lift with bags in hand.

***

"I'm going to have to see some ID before letting you in."

Barely reaching the height of Carter's shoulder, a doctor blocked the doorway to the resort's mortuary. He made a show of examining their credentials before reluctantly standing aside.

"My name's Dr Mostrek. I apologise for the formalities, however security is necessarily tight at the moment. If just one photo of the victims hits the internet, Silver-Trust's big launch will be left in tatters."

Carter trailed the doctor into the room, shaking his head in surprise at the man's priorities. In the centre was an examination trolley overhung by a pedestal light. One end of the room was filled by a large silver mortuary fridge, while the other had a bench and cupboards holding an array of surgical equipment.

"Two dead bodies, and your biggest concern is the resort's launch? Could have sworn you were a medic, not an event planner," said Carter.

"Very funny, Agent," said Mostrek without hint of a smile. "I may be a doctor, but I'm cognisant of who pays my wage. Silver-Trust's circle of influence is larger than most, and I'd prefer to not be blacklisted."

"Please excuse my colleague's lack of manners," said Rylan, fixing Carter with a glare. "What he's failed to consider is your responsibility to maintain confidentiality of the deceased, and your duty to the families who wouldn't want strangers ogling their loved ones for mere curiosity."

Carter put up his hands in mute apology, and took a step back.

Agent Rylan approached the steel cabinets. "I'm somewhat surprised the resort has a mortuary. Convenient for us, but unusual all the same."

The doctor nodded, his features relaxing at Rylan's intervention. "In our European resorts, we have many rich clients who are determined to hit the slopes despite being, how shall I say, in less than peak physical condition. Invariably, a few suffer heart attacks and cannot be revived. As such, it's necessary to store the bodies until they can be retrieved."

He walked to the mortuary fridge, opened a square door at waist height and slid out a steel bench. On top was the first victim, the corpse wrapped in a blue body bag. With a frown, he unzipped the bag from head to waist, exposing a woman. The corpse was still dressed, the shirt and jumper roughly cut up the centre to expose the chest for initial assessment.

"They found Trish first."

Carter joined the other two and stared down at the victim. "Did you know her?"

"Only by sight. There's so many people working in the lodge, it's near impossible to know them all well."

Her eyes were open, staring blindly at the ceiling. Skin was pale, but unmarked. Rylan pulled on a set of plastic gloves before touching the victim's neck.

"Jesus, she's frozen solid."

"Her body was out in the open, at least forty paces off the track and half covered by snow. Quite lucky to be found really. When someone goes missing in a snow storm, the body often remains hidden until the spring melt. One of the search party caught a glimpse of her jacket poking out of the snow."

Rylan gently moved parts of the clothes, looking for signs of trauma. "I don't see any wounds or bites. Was hypothermia the cause of death?"

Mostrek gave a brisk nod of affirmation. "Unfortunately, the second body is in much worse condition."

Rylan stood back, allowing the doctor to open a second door and slide out the next victim. Carter pulled on a set of gloves as well, and helped her to unzip the body bag.

"Bloody hell…" said Carter under his breath.

It was hardly the first macerated corpse he'd seen. Once a body lay in the sun for a day or two and the bloat kicked in, nothing beautiful of the human condition remained. But this was different.

"What the hell happened to him?"

The body was dismembered, parts totally missing. The legs had been severed at the hips, arms at the shoulders. The femurs were missing, while the lower legs had been stripped of calf muscles, leaving the bone and feet behind. Upper arms and shoulders were missing, however, forearms stripped of muscle accompanied the body. The abdomen was sliced open at the right upper quadrant, the overlying skin and muscle hanging inwards as if it was hollowed out underneath.

The doctor looked up at the agents. "I was hoping the two of you might be able to shed some light. I've never seen anything like it."

Rylan dragged a pedestal light from the room's corner and directed a light beam onto the shoulder. Leaning close, she ran a fingertip over the edge of the amputation.

"Here the wound is clean, like it was incised by a surgeon's blade. And yet at other locations," she said, pointing to a different wound, "there are definite teeth marks. It makes no sense for them to exist on the same corpse." Rylan stood back, chewing her bottom lip as she stared at the remains.

"There's something else you should probably see," said the doctor. "If you'd help me turn the body over?"

Carter took a grip at torso and pelvis, and rolled the corpse to its side.

"The buttocks and muscles of the lower back have been stripped, and if you check the mouth," the doctor said, indicating for Carter to lay the body back down, "do you see anything missing?"

Rylan shone the light into the mouth as Mostrek levered open the jaw. "The tongue's sliced out at the root."

"Almost looks like he's been butchered, removing the prime cuts of meat," said Carter.

Rylan glanced up, and for the first time he noted a touch of respect to her gaze. "I think you might be on to something. Can you spread that abdominal wound wide for me?"

Carter raised an eyebrow, but when he realised she was serious, he pulled up his sleeves and tentatively sunk his fingers in.

"No, I mean properly. Grab hold of each side of the abdominal wall, muscles and all, and spread them."

Carter tasted sour bile at the back of his throat as he complied. Unlike the first body, this one had been found in the shed and avoided freezing outright, but not by much. The muscles gave a slight crunch, like steak put in the freezer to stiffen before carving into strips for jerky.

Rylan shone a pen torch into the wound, then shoved her hand and forearm deep into the cavity, reaching up into the chest. "Thought as much."

The doctor gagged as she pulled her arm out with a slurp, and Carter let the sides of the wound go. Blood and fatty goo striped the skin of her arm above the redundant glove. Rylan flicked her gloves into a bin then scrubbed her forearms and hands at a basin in the far corner.

"Carter, after you mentioned butchering, the wound to the abdomen and tongue made more sense."

"How's that?"

"Organs such as the liver are nutrient rich with high concentrations of certain vitamins. As such, they are prized by many predatory animals. In this man, his liver, heart, and probably pancreas, are all missing."

"What about the tongue?" asked Carter.

"Sometimes Orca will slaughter a whale, eating only the tongue and liver, the parts they enjoy the most, while leaving the rest of the carcass for scavengers. Maybe whatever killed him was also fond of the tongue?"

"All of this doesn't tell us what killed the man," said Carter.

"At minimum, it shows it had some degree of intelligence. Knowing how to dismember a carcass to gain the largest cuts of meat and choice organs," said Rylan. "What sort of animal is capable of such a thing?"

"Easy. A human," said Carter. "There are records of cannibalistic killers across the world. We've just found the next freak with an appetite for his fellow man."

"True. It could be multiple generations of a single family, executing murders across two centuries."

Carter gave a silent sigh of relief. If Rylan wouldn't consider rationale explanations, then he was going to have a hard time staying employed.

"But that doesn't change the current situation. The resort launches tomorrow, releasing hundreds of skiers onto unguarded remote trails. Whether we have a human or animal predator on the loose, this race needs to be postponed and guests kept indoors."

Rylan turned to Dr Mostrek. "Who do I need to speak with to call off the race?"

The doctor sighed. "You've got a snowflake's chance in hell, Agent. Silver-Trust's CEO is here for the opening. Jacob Freidman arrived yesterday."

"Freidman? I thought he owned a pharmaceutical company?" said Carter.

"As I said earlier. Silver-Trust's circle of influence is wide, with interests stretching across many industries. The pharmaceutical side of the business is mostly involved in research at this stage, but it's shown promising advances that may see it become one of the big players in the industry," said Mostrek.

"Hence why you want to keep your boss onside, eh?"

Mostrek shrugged. "Clinical work is mentally and physically draining. I wouldn't be the first to consider a research post for the right amount of money." The doctor's gaze shifted back to Rylan. "Hey, what the hell do you think you're doing?"

Rylan ignored him and finished off slicing a small section of tissue from a bite wound to place in a test tube.

"These bodies are going to the coroner, they shouldn't have anything removed!"

"I don't know what you're talking about." Rylan slipped the tube into the pocket of her coat with practiced sleight of hand. "But, before you make such an accusation, I would ask how a respected doctor such as yourself allowed a body under their care to be compromised. I imagine Mr Freidman would be unimpressed."

Mostrek glared at her, lips narrowed. "As pleasurable as this conversation has been, I have a clinic to open." He zipped up the body bags and slid them into the fridge before pointing at the door. "If you would be so kind as to leave, *now*."

CHAPTER THREE

Carter hung back, following a few steps behind Agent Rylan and their escort to Freidman's office. The hotel atrium was huge, vaulted ceiling reaching three storeys above the tiles. Carter glanced upward, his gaze drawn to chandelier inspired light pieces, each probably worth more than his yearly wage. A few guests leaned over the rail of a mezzanine level high above with champagne glasses in hand, lazily people watching the crowd below. The hotel's restaurant opened off the right side of the foyer, wait staff hurriedly adding the finishing touches to tables ahead of the evening bookings; while to the left, a bar and café area was packed to bursting. Every surface sparkled, not a speck of dust or a smudge to be seen. Carter's gaze roved over the lot, automatically cataloguing the layout, places to take cover and means of egress. He grunted in annoyance at himself. This was Australia, not the bloody Middle East, but old habits from years in the field died hard.

As they approached the lift doors, Rylan pointed at a Monet on the wall. Accentuated by a series of subtle lights, the 'Houses of Parliament' painting was kept safely cordoned out of reach. She leant over the rope, mouth slightly open as her gaze explored the canvas.

"Freidman's going all out to impress. It would have cost him a fortune to lease it from the Musée d'Orsay."

Carter grunted, unimpressed. "Looks like the artist spilled his paint set over the canvas."

"It's supposed to be sunrise through the fog. You know, just because you shoot a gun, doesn't mean you can't appreciate art."

"Each to their own," Carter shrugged. "People find beauty in different places. I'd rather be outdoors in nature than gazing at an old painting, not that there's much of it left. You know, we lost 400,000 hectares of alpine forest to bushfire the other year — that's forest that's never burnt before — and Silver-Trust has magnified those losses by clearing additional bushland to build these bloody ski runs."

"I didn't realise you were an environmentalist."

Now it was Carter's turn to raise an eyebrow. "Just because I'm an ex-soldier, doesn't mean I'm a card-carrying conservative either. There might be a few preconceptions of your own to fix."

Before she could answer, the doors of the lift opened. "If you would come this way, ma'am," said the porter, ushering them inside before selecting the top floor. "Mr Freidman will be along very soon."

The agents were taken past two penthouse suits to Freidman's private apartment and shown into an empty meeting room. A large wooden desk and tall-backed leather armchair presided over the room, dwarfing the two smaller seats for visitors. The eastern wall was made entirely of glass, granting panoramic views of the snow-cloaked highlands. Two stationary chairlifts snaked their way up the nearest empty slope. Come the morning, they would stutter to life and begin carrying Silver-Trust's rich clients up the mountain.

Turning away from the view, Rylan extracted a laptop from her satchel, opened the computer on Freidman's desk and brought up a black and white photo. She hooked a finger at Carter, calling him closer for a look.

"As far as I can tell, the murders commenced with this man, a settler named Ian Rankin."

Carter peered over her shoulder at the image. The photo was ancient and badly faded with water damage at the base. The photo's subject stared seriously from the screen, frown lines carved deep into his brow. A thick moustache curved from his upper lip almost reaching the chin, while two lambchop sideburns kissed his jawline. The date, March 1867, was hand written at the bottom.

"After immigrating from Scotland, Rankin was amongst the first settlers to begin grazing cattle in the highlands. His main land holding was where the small town of Mt. Beauty now lies, but during the summer months his cattle would graze the highland pastures."

Rylan brought up a national park map on the screen and indicated the location of an old building. "Like a number of graziers, he built himself a hut to live within while fattening his cattle. In 1870, the Mansfield Times paper noted his remains were found in the small building. Although no description of the body was provided, it stated that the corpse was in 'poor shape'."

"That could just mean it was heavily decomposed," said Carter.

"Possibly. However, in 1900 when the next killings occur, the paper clearly states that the two men's bodies were hacked apart." Rylan closed the screen and sat back in one of the small chairs. "Every thirty years since, a violent killing has been recorded within twenty kilometres of Rankin's Hut, matching the pattern of our victim today.

"Now, if these killings are due to humans, that would require an unprecedented level of communication, cooperation and dedication across multiple generations. Surely, at some point there would have been a person who refused to take part, or on the opposite end of the spectrum, a killer that escalated."

Carter grunted acknowledgment. "And if the murders are unrelated, it would be nigh on impossible for them to occur at regimented thirty year intervals." He saw the slightest hint of a smile from his partner.

"It's why I became interested in the case," said Rylan. "Are there any animals that can survive long periods of time without feeding, maybe in a state of hibernation?"

Carter walked to the window, stared at the snow laden gums on the mountain side and shoved his hands into his pockets. "I didn't think there were any Australian animals that did that?"

"There's a handful," said Rylan. "Echidnas will hibernate if they have a territory above the snowline, while the mountain pygmy possum can exist in a torpor for up to five months. But hibernation isn't all related to snow. There are frogs in central Australia that can exist beneath the mud during drought periods for years at a time."

"I know the energy needs of hibernation would be miniscule compared to an active animal, but they'd still eventually run out of fat stores. Surely there's no precedent for a thirty year period of hibernation?"

"Okay, let's park the hibernation idea," said Rylan. "Maybe we're looking at a lifecycle event?"

The door suddenly swung inwards, admitting two men. The first made straight for the seat behind the large desk, while the second closed the door and took up a position behind the agents.

"My name's Jacob Freidman," said the man behind the desk. Looking somewhere in his fifties, an already balding head was shaved close to the skin. He wore a tailor-cut navy suit. Middle-age spread softened his belly, straining the buttons of his shirt as he sat. Despite the coolness of the room, sweat prickled across his brow as his gaze flicked between the two agents with unguarded irritation. "I will start by saying my time is incredibly short, there is much to organise prior to the launch."

"Two of your staff have been murdered, and..." started Rylan before Freidman cut her off.

"Yes. And Dr Mostrek informs me you think an undiscovered species with extreme longevity is responsible," he sneered. "Why's ASIO wasting money on hunting shadows instead of finding the real killer?"

Rylan's jaw clenched briefly, but she managed to keep her tone neutral. "We follow the evidence wherever it goes, Mr Freidman. We aim to bring the killer to justice, while maintaining the safety of the public. And unfortunately, whatever slaughtered your employee is still on the loose."

"Your point?"

"I request that you delay the opening of the resort, and cancel the cross-country ski event until the killer is brought to ground," said Rylan.

Freidman let out a bark of laughter, his face devoid of humour. "Did you hear that, Ash?"

Carter glanced over his shoulder at the man behind him. Standing at least six-foot-four inches, Carter had met his type before. Generally ex-special services, instead of re-entering civilian life on retirement, they chose to enter the world of private military contractors. Of dubious legality, they were essentially mercenaries who sold their services to the highest bidder.

"I think they're dreaming," said Ash in a broad English accent. "We can't be cancelling events, boss, just because these twats think there's an angry fucking unicorn or something hiding in the bush."

Freidman smirked. "Unless of course, you can provide me hard evidence that this isn't just a murder committed by some deranged lunatic?"

"It is early in the investigation. We've been on site for less than three hours," said Rylan.

"I'll take that as a no," said Freidman, voice dripping with condescension. "As agreed prior, you are welcome within my resort, but please, do not bother me again with baseless theories." He turned to his guard. "Ash, could you please see them out."

Seeing no other avenue to pursue, Carter and Rylan allowed themselves to be shown back to the hallway.

"That went well," said Carter in a low voice as they walked back to the lift. "His guard Ash was a merc, for sure. I'd say probably ex-British army."

"If he wants to pander to a rich arsehole, that's his business."

"Nah, I reckon there's more to it," said Carter. "You don't employ a guard dog of that quality unless you've got some serious security fears."

"And you don't make billions of dollars without creating a few enemies," said Rylan with a shrug. "But we've got our own issues. If Freidman won't cooperate, I want to get a look at the hut where the attack happened. Maybe we can find enough evidence to force his hand."

Carter glanced at his watch. "It'll have to wait until first light tomorrow; dusk's in thirty minutes. The risk of hypothermia's too high. Neither of us know the bush here, all it would take is one wrong turn in the dark and we'd be popsicles."

***

"What do you think?" asked Freidman. "Is it worth pursuing?"

Ash glanced up from the computer screen for a moment and saw the greedy hunger in his employer's eye.

"I hate to say it, but their story checks out. There's been a death bang on every thirty years. Bloody strange. If it is from the one beast, it'll be the longest living land creature ever found. Studying how it prevents cellular degradation for such periods of time might provide a breakthrough for your senolytics study."

Freidman pulled a bottle of whiskey from a cupboard under his desk and poured a finger of amber liquid into two glasses, passing one to Ash. "If it does, it'll save our neck. There's been little progress to date, not enough to satisfy our board. But if we can replicate such longevity in a human subject, we could charge whatever we wanted for the treatment and people would pay." He downed the spirit in one gulp before slapping Ash on the shoulder.

"Whatever it is, I want first option. Follow them and if the beast is real, get to it first. If it's found on Silver-Trust land, it belongs to us anyway. Don't let me down."

The soldier stood, the first stirrings of excitement speeding his heart. If it came to a fight with the ASIO agents, he was going to have some fun.

CHAPTER FOUR

High above Nicole's head, a stationary four-seater ski lift hung from a thick cable. As she glanced up, a blast of freezing air set the chair swaying. Since she and her partner Alex had started their hike in the early afternoon, the temperature had dropped markedly—not that it worried her. They'd been hiking the Australian High Country for the better part of twenty years, and came well prepared for any change in weather. Nestled under multiple layers of clothes, with thick gloves and beanie keeping her hands and head warm, Nicole was comfortable despite walking through ankle-deep snow.

Not wanting to see the tree-lopping in process, the pair had stayed away from the area until Silver-Trust had completed construction of their alpine resort. Their current hiking trail snaked back and forth through Silver-Trust land. Although access to the path was still freely available, it brought walkers in contact with the changes wrought on the scenery.

Alex pulled up for a moment to adjust his pack and shoulder straps. While she waited, Nicole bent down to brush the snow off a tree stump at the edge of the path. The installation of the ski-lift had required the cutting of trees, old growth forest that had never felt the bite of a chainsaw. The tip of her gloved finger traced rings upon the stump slowly inward, her lips silently counting.

"This tree was over a hundred years old, Alex," she said, her face downcast. "Surely they could have let it remain and just lopped the highest branches? It's old trees like this that provide the hollows needed for animals to nest. Where are they supposed go now?"

Nicole was an active member of a conservation group to protect the mountain pygmy-possum, and although that animal favoured boulder fields and rocky scree, she was mindful of the other alpine animals that needed the trees for survival.

Alex rested a hand on her shoulder for a moment, giving it a brief squeeze before moving on again. Nicole hadn't really expected a response, knowing her husband was just as disappointed. Another twenty paces took them away from the cleared slope and ski-lift, and back under the branches of snow gum as the trail curled off to the east, back into the national park.

"How much farther to Rankin's Hut?" asked Nicole. The last time she'd walked this trail was over five years before.

"Not far, maybe ten minutes," said Alex, then pointed to something off the trail. "We've made it to the 'Three Brothers', should be over the next ridge."

Nicole followed Alex's direction, a sense of unease coiling in her gut as she stared at the rock formation. Three upright pillars of stone sprouted from the ground, each with vaguely human features, as if tall men had been turned to rock and weathered by thousands of years. In the afternoon's fading light, green lichen grew across the tallest figure's face in a malformed smile. "I'd forgotten how creepy they were."

Alex barked a short laugh. "Rocks can't be *creepy*, my love."

"I guess not, but sometimes locations have an awful feeling to them, as if the ground has been stained by evil." As they walked past them, Nicole glanced back at the stone formation. "Maybe something awful happened here, a death or murder perhaps?"

"Don't tell me you're going to start telling ghost stories around the campfire tonight."

"You know, for a passable husband, you can be a dick sometimes," said Nicole rolling her eyes. "*Lots* of shit happened all over the country back in the 1800s. Indigenous people were massacred during the Frontier Wars, and I'd wager a few crimes were committed by early settlers against each other."

Alex raised his hands in mock surrender. "Okay, I know you take this sort of stuff seriously, but until I see a ghost myself, saying things like 'evil can stain a place' is always going to make me laugh."

"What about when you walked through the grounds of the Broad Arrow Café at Port Arthur? You said it felt like wading into a pool of cold water."

Alex shrugged. "Yeah, but I already knew it was the site of a mass killing. That's just my subconscious affecting my senses, nothing more." He glanced away, obviously keen to change the subject. "Look, there's the hut up ahead. We've got three nights out in the snow while we're on this walk. Do you want to use it, or pitch the tent?"

Rankin's Hut loomed at the edge of the trail. A simple building from the 1800s, it had walls of desiccated timber panels, paint curling off the wood in psoriatic flakes of white. Two small windows stared out from under a narrow veranda with a psychopathic flat gaze. The roof was rusted corrugated iron and probably leaking. It had been taken over by park rangers and repurposed as emergency accommodation for hikers decades earlier, but little maintenance appeared to have occurred. Nicole climbed the steps and swung open the front door, the hinge complaining with a high-pitched squeal. Stale air wafted out of the single room, carrying a faint odour of decay.

She grimaced, closed the door again and joined her husband back on the snow. "As much as I can't be arsed pitching the tent, I don't want to sleep in there. It smells damp and is probably infested with bed bugs. We'll stink and itch for the rest of the trek."

Alex sighed, then unclipped the top of his pack to extract their tent. "All right. At least the building will give us a little shelter from the wind if it doesn't change direction."

***

"Hey babe, come and have a look at this," said Nicole.

Now that the tent was up and a small feed of two-minute noodles finished, she'd wandered to the edge of the tree line with a mug of hot tea cradled in her gloves. The light had all but disappeared, just a glow remaining above the western ridge. Shadows cast by the snow gums reached across the snow like vast claws. The wind of earlier had faded with the light, leaving an unnatural silence in its wake. With a twist of her hand, she turned on her head torch and aimed the beam down at the ground where a wide hole descended beneath the earth.

What the hell made you, I wonder?

Approximately a metre in diameter, the tunnel shelved down into the earth at a steep angle. Twice the size of any wombat hole she'd seen, it had freshly excavated dirt around it. To the right, blood had melted the snow to a crimson slurry.

Heavy steps crunched through the snow behind her and Nicole glanced back to see Alex approaching. "What is it?"

She shrugged. "A den of some sort? What do you reckon made it?"

Alex crouched and shined a pen torch onto the bloodied area. "Don't know, but it's carnivorous." His torch beam paused, highlighting a blue bit of fabric. His picked it up, rolled it between his fingers before flicking it away again. "Some poor rabbit or wallaby met its end, I reckon. Nothing to worry for us, though. Dingoes and wild dogs tend to give humans a wide berth in this area."

He walked back to their small two-man tent, Nicole trailing a few steps behind. The last minutes of dusk bled away, leaving a crescent moon to illuminate the slopes.

Alex bent to unzip the tent. "Call it a night?"

Nicole flicked the last of her tea onto the ground and turned her head torch off, ready to follow her partner into the tent. A crunch of feet on snow sounded from the edge of the clearing. Nicole froze mid-movement and turned to scan the tree line. She waited for her eyes to adjust to the lower light; trees, branches and rock slowly emerging from the gloom. A low moan of a breeze through branches wavered in the air, then nothing.

Silence.

Footsteps crunched again, this time to the right, past the hut. Nicole's heart stuttered, hairs rising on the back of her neck. A moving shadow froze in the far trees, the footsteps ceasing at the same time.

"Alex?" she whispered. "I think there's something watching us." At the slight wobble in her voice, her husband's head poked out of the tent.

"Hello? Anyone out there?" he shouted. Alex's voice echoed across the landscape, bouncing off boulders, returning from myriad directions at once. He looked up at his wife, annoyance creasing his forehead. "What did you see?"

"I don't know." She scanned the slope, starting to feel a little silly. "There was something moving in the trees over there, but now I can't see it."

Alex withdrew into the tent again, grumbling something unintelligible under his breath.

Probably a wallaby.

Nicole silently cursed herself for raising the story of the Port Arthur massacre. When nylon fabric was all that stood between you and a murderer's knife, it was stupid to talk about psycho killers. Guaranteed, she'd be having nightmares all night.

She zipped the tent door behind her, shimmied into her sleeping bag and spooned up against Alex for added warmth. An arm's length above, the tent shuddered in the breeze. Her husband threw an arm over her and gave her a squeeze.

"Nothing to worry about, babe. Let's get some shut eye, then make it a new day tomorrow, yeah?"

Footsteps crunched up the slope coming towards their tent at pace, setting Nicole's pulse racing again. Breath tight in her chest, she shrank back against Alex. "You had to have heard it that time?"

Alex ripped open his sleeping bag, brows furrowed with anger as he pulled on hiking boots and a jacket. "I'm getting royally sick of this shit," he muttered, unzipping the tent door and climbing out. The nylon flapped behind him in the wind, obstructing her view.

"Oi, you!" shouted Alex. "What the fuck do you think you're playing at? If you want to use the hut, you're welcome to it, but stop running around in the dark. You're starting to scare my wife."

"What's happening out there?" asked Nicole, an edge to her voice.

"Nothing, babe. Just some other hiker being a dick. I'll be back in a minute once I sort them out."

Alex's footsteps receded from the tent and she heard a faint click as he turned his torch on. "*Jesus... No*."

Suddenly, Alex was sprinting back toward their tent, a strangled cry of terror in his throat. Nicole pulled aside the tent door to see better. Alex had lost his torch, and a black figure closed in from behind. It was huge, at least seven feet tall, long arms reaching for her husband.

"Nicole, RUN!" he screamed.

Alex stumbled, foot catching on a snow-covered tussock, and then it was on him. Nicole zipped the door back up as Alex's first scream tortured her ears. She whimpered, limbs like jelly, unable to move, her brain frozen like a rabbit in the spotlight. There was a wet tearing sound followed by splattering liquid, and finally her husband fell silent.

Footsteps approached the tent again, this time slow and measured until they stopped outside. Nicole shrank against the rear wall, holding a trekking pole in a white knuckled grip. Suddenly, a razor-sharp talon punctured the nylon, slicing a long rent in the fabric.

Nicole's breath caught in her chest. Although vaguely humanoid in shape, it wasn't a man that stood outside. An arm stabbed through the hole, gripped her ankle with bony fingers and tore her through the gap onto the snow.

Nicole finally found her voice, a cry of terror shredding her vocal cords like a bandsaw. She kicked with her free leg but with every strike, it felt like she was hitting steel-plate. Ignoring her efforts, the creature tugged her down the slope, past her husband's corpse towards the hole in the earth. She gouged runnels in the snow in an attempt to stop the beast's progress, fingernails splintering on rocks under the white mantle.

Within moments, they reached the edge of the tunnel. Her belly dragged over the lip and then she was going down, feet first to the black depths underground. As the star-filled sky was finally blacked out, Nicole screamed.

CHAPTER FIVE

Carter reached out a gloved hand to trace a gouge in the shed wall. Four deep scrapes had cut deep, almost penetrating the sheet metal. The panel showed signs that it had been buckled, however the worst of the dints were pushed back out. A black object was stuck at the base of one scratch. Carter used the tip of his pocketknife to lever it out, then dropped it into a plastic bag before holding it up to the light for a better view.

That ain't from a human.

Jet-black and shiny, a two centimetre length of talon lay in the evidence bag.

"Fucking idiots have destroyed everything of use," said Rylan from inside the shed. "I'm used to forensics messing with my scene, but losing out to civilians really gets my back up."

A maintenance team had cleaned the murder scene the previous day, readying the shed for the cross-country ski race. Rylan had banged on Carter's door an hour before dawn, keen to use every minute of daylight. With the starters gun due to fire in less than an hour, they had little time to stop the race. And it wouldn't be just the competitors at risk, soon the chairlifts would creak into life, flooding the downhill runs with skiers. Carter pocketed the evidence bag and joined his partner inside the shed.

Rylan stood in the centre of the room with hands on hips, biting her bottom lip as she stared at the ground. "The body was dismembered there," she said, pointing out a dark stain. "They've used bleach on the bloodstain, but did a shit job. Obviously haven't dealt with a trauma cleaning before."

Carter turned back to the doorway. The lock was new, maintenance having installed a temporary slide latch and padlock to replace the broken mechanism.

"Did you find anything outside?" asked Rylan.

"Maybe." Carter handed over the piece of talon. "It was stuck at the bottom of a scratch in the door. I did a lap of the shed and their ute, but didn't see any more clues. The weather hasn't helped much," he said with a grimace. "Fresh snow fell overnight, everything's covered."

The low rumble of an approaching vehicle grabbed Carter's attention and he stepped outside to see a battered Land Rover with National Park insignia pull to a halt beside their rented SUV. A bloke climbed out of the driver's seat, zipping up a thick jacket over his uniform before heading their way.

"You expecting anyone?" Carter asked over his shoulder.

"If it's a park ranger, then yes." She stepped around Carter and waved the man inside. "Martin, thanks for joining us."

"Agent Rylan, I take it?" asked the ranger.

Rylan nodded, shaking his hand. "And this is Agent Carter," she said, nodding in Eoin's direction.

The ranger gave Carter an easy smile, deep lines around his eyes crinkling in welcome. He pulled off his beanie and scratched at his scalp. "First time I've been in one of these new storage sheds." Martin's gaze dropped to the blood-stained concrete, his smile fading. "I heard what happened, pretty awful stuff. My boss said you had some questions about the area's history?"

"Are there any stories of a killer that emerges periodically? Maybe even before Europeans colonised this area?" asked Rylan.

Martin leaned against the hut wall, a small cloud of steam coming from his mouth in the frigid air as he sighed. "Yeah, people talk. I wouldn't vouch for the degree of truth to them, probably no more than campfire stories to scare kids. Fact gets diluted by fiction with every retelling," he said with a shrug.

Rylan kept eye contact, her face serious. "But in most stories, there's *a kernel* of truth."

Martin eyed her for a moment longer, then shrugged as if coming to a decision. "All right. But if you want the story, we should probably head to where the modern part of it began."

***

Carter followed the ranger and Rylan off the narrow walking track and into a clearing dominated by an ancient settler's hut. Due east of the resource shed and ski field, it had taken a ten minute drive, followed by fifteen minutes trudging along a narrow walking trail to reach the location.

"That's Rankin's Hut," said Martin, pointing up at the dilapidated building. "Built by its namesake back in 1868."

Melt water dripped from a rusted corrugated iron roof. Built of hand cut wooden panels, age had warped and split many of the boards. The blue sky of earlier was gone, grey clouds now crowding the sky to the horizon. Carter felt something cold and wet on his cheek and glanced up to see snowflakes tossed by the breeze as they sifted gently to the ground.

"Let's talk inside," said Martin.

Cold musty air enveloped Carter as he followed the others into the hut. He brushed snow off his shoulders to melt on the floor and shivered. If anything, it seemed almost colder inside. Martin flicked a yellowed plastic light switch next to the door. A naked bulb hanging from the rafters blinked into light, bathing the room in a purulent yellow glow. The hut was small, less than ten paces from one side to the other. The original brick hearth was centred in one of the walls, although a permanent steel mesh had been bolted across the fireplace to prevent its use. A set of wooden bunks hunched in one corner, the only other furniture being a plastic-topped kitchen table ringed by tall-backed seats and a threadbare couch.

Carter rubbed at one of the dirty windows, trying to clear a patch to see outside while Rylan pulled out one of the chairs from the table and took a seat. "Okay, you've got us here, what's the story?"

Martin took one of the other chairs for himself, his gaze turned inward for a few moments until he looked up at both of the agents.

"There's a reason this hut is run down. Although it's one of the oldest in the park and deserving of upkeep, you'll be hard pressed to get any ranger to come here alone, let alone stay the night. Few hikers use it. After sticking their heads inside, most elect to keep walking or sleep outside in their tents."

"Bit odd," said Carter. "I'd prefer a dry room over bivouacking any day of the year."

"Yeah, I think it's one of those gut feelings that people don't explore too deeply," said Martin with an uneasy grin. "Most just want to be gone."

"You said this place was built in 1868?" asked Rylan, redirecting the conversation.

The ranger nodded. "Colin Rankin was a Scottish settler who claimed the land despite the region already being inhabited. The resident Indigenous people warned him the area was a spiritual site and not safe to build upon. They believed this mountain belonged to ravenous souls, spirits that rose once a lifetime to feast on the living. Any person unlucky enough to cross the path of a hungry spirit would be dragged to their lair beneath the ground."

"What's the name of these 'spirits'?" asked Rylan.

"The Indigenous people referred to them by numerous names, however, the most common once translated to English is simply a 'Soul Feeder'. Truly glutinous, they feed not only on flesh, but stories said they derive as much sustenance from their victims' terror prior to death."

Carter glanced at the surrounding walls of the hut. "Well, it seems Rankin ignored their advice," said Carter.

"Worse," said Martin with a grimace. "The bastard repaid the information with murder, gifting the tribe a sack of flour laced with arsenic. Men, women and children died in agony, killed like vermin. The local troopers turned a blind eye, as they did to most atrocities against the Indigenous population. And so, Colin Rankin took the land and built his house. A small one room shack to stand against the elements.

"He should have listened to the elder's warning. Within two years, Rankin disappeared, never to be seen again. Since then, death has haunted the spot. Another two settlers went missing after claiming the hut as their own." Martin scratched at his neck, his eyes flitting around the room, drawn to each shadow as if searching for something within. "After that, it was given up by the locals as 'cursed', left empty until the national park thought to use it for an emergency hut for hikers in bad weather. And yet still the deaths continue. Seems to be every twenty or thirty years, a hiker or two goes missing while walking in this region."

"Every thirty years, to be precise," said Rylan. "And always in the first month of winter."

Martin shrugged. "Like I said, it's just a story to me. I always figured they'd walked off a cliff in the dark, or become disorientated with hypothermia and left the trail. Either way, despite its beauty, I could think of a million other places I'd rather go for a walk."

"I saw deep scratch marks in the metal door of the storage shed," said Carter. "What sort of animals could do such a thing? We were thinking maybe a dingo or wild dog, but I also found an article online claiming a large black cat had been seen in the local bushland?"

Martin laughed. "Nah, there's no pumas or leopards around here."

"Hundreds of Australian towns have claimed the presence of a large black cat at some point, but I've found no evidence to give the tales credence," said Rylan.

"People forget how large a well-fed feral cat can grow in the wild," said Martin. "Now dingoes and wild dogs, they're another thing. But by the time the first snow has fallen, they've long retreated to lower altitudes of their hunting territory. Short story, I've got no idea what sort of animal could have done those scratches."

Carter grit his teeth. They were getting nowhere with this, chasing myths when they should be looking for a hillbilly killer or scouring the crime scene for DNA. He needed some fresh air to think.

"I'm going to take a look around outside. That okay with you, boss?"

Rylan didn't even look up from her pad of paper as she scribbled notes from the ranger's story, just gave him a curt nod. Carter pulled up the hood of his jacket and closed the hut door carefully behind himself. Snow continued to gently fall as he left Rylan to finish her interview of the ranger.

Trees had been cleared about the hut, leaving fifty metres of open ground in all directions. Snow humped over tussocks of grass, like a white blanket had been thrown to hide the toys of his children at home. A frown darkened his features as he considered how long it would be until he saw his kids again. Carter had two daughters with his ex-wife, aged six and nine. They'd spent far too much of their childhood growing up without a father. He'd leave for a six month tour of duty, and return to kids that had grown inches and achieved massive developmental improvements.

All without his help.

With so many deployments, his wife Kim had learnt to live without him, and now found it easier when he didn't get in the way. He'd seen her love for him fade, then morph from bitterness to indifference, and had felt powerless to change it. Not when the next tour of duty was always around the corner. Kim had asked him to quit, but in his head that was never an option. If Carter didn't go back overseas, who else would protect his mates when the shit hit the fan? If his fellow soldiers still faced risk, then he knew his place was to help shoulder the burden. He'd thought she'd understand, after all, Carter had been a soldier when they met. Instead, he'd learnt that distance rarely makes the heart grow fonder.

And then the army had dumped him anyway.

Now all he had to show for his national servic, was two daughters that barely knew him, a hip full of shrapnel and a head full of nightmares.

What a fucking joke.

He spat a sour taste from his mouth and began to walk around to the back of the hut, following trail markers toward the bush.

As he passed the corner of the building, he stopped dead. A few paces behind the hut, an orange tent stood drunkenly, slashed nylon fluttering in the breeze. In a heartbeat his Glock was in hand, eyes scanning the clearing and trees, searching for a combatant to engage. A familiar surge of adrenaline infused his chest, heart rate increasing, erasing fatigue in an instant. If he was honest, there was a part of battle he'd missed, a peculiar excitement mixed with fear that left normal life a pale shadow.

Seeing nothing, he surged up to the tent, nudging aside the torn fabric with the tip of his handgun to see inside. It was empty of life. Dark blood soaked the sleeping bags within, the contents of the tent left torn and dishevelled. Crimson streaked the nylon wall below the cut fabric, and as Carter turned his head, he realised that there was a slight depression in the snow heading down the slope where something had been dragged. Although falling snow had softened the appearance, the route taken was clear.

"Rylan, I need you out here!"

He ran down the slope, staying to the right of the depression to avoid damaging the tracks. Closer to the tree line, his legs sunk almost to his knees in a drift, and then he saw it. A wide hole disappeared into the earth, sloping back into the hill at a steep angle. Gore had soaked the snow and dirt at the entrance to an abattoir's slurry of red mud. He pulled a small Maglite torch from his pocket, squatted, and twisted on the beam. The tunnel extended straight for two metres, then bent to the left, blocking any further view. At the turn, he saw the toe of an empty hiking boot lying in the dirt.

Shit.

Rylan slid to a stop at his side, gun in hand, face flushed. "Is anyone in that tent?"

Carter shook his head. "Empty. I followed drag marks to this hole."

Rylan grabbed his shoulder. "Did you hear that?"

Carter knelt, ear to the hole. A muffled scream sounded, faint within the depths of the hill.

Jesus, they're still alive!

He holstered his Glock, then quickly stripped off his thick jacket to decrease bulk, passing it to the ranger who'd also arrived.

"You're not seriously thinking of crawling in there?" asked Martin, his face pale.

Carter gave a curt nod. He didn't want to think about it, just knew it had to be done. He could handle fighting through jungle, or room to room in a broken city, but hated following an enemy underground with a passion. He'd lost more than a few mates chasing Taliban into their mountain caves. Underground, any bullet strike or explosion could set off a tunnel collapse, burying you alive under tonnes of dirt and rock. There was no coming back from such a thing. You could only hope that the crush killed you instantly. He didn't want to starve alone in the darkness with nothing but pain for company.

Carter looked up at Rylan. "Can you two search for any other tunnel exits?"

She nodded. "If it becomes too tight to move safely, come straight back out."

"What do you think this will be?" Carter ran through a quick weapons check, before laying on his belly. Blood-stained slush soaked his jumper, coating his belly in an icy slick.

Rylan bit her lip, looking like she was about to say something before shaking her head. "Not sure."

Great.

He forced a deep breath, turned his focus ahead and entered the tunnel. The ceiling lowered at the first bend, leaving little more than a handspan above his back. There would be no space to turn around. Carter forced himself onwards, leopard crawling with torch in one hand, Glock in the other. Sharp stones protruded from the dirt walls and floor, gouging scarlet runnels in his skin.

Another scream sounded, a heart-rending wail of agony that abruptly cut off with a wet crunch. Suddenly, the roof arched upward into the dark, providing ample room to stand. Carter drew his legs underneath, gaining his feet once more. The narrow confines of the tunnel had opened into a cavernous space, large enough that his torch beam failed to reach the far end.

He turned on the spot, shining the torch beside his handgun, heart thumping like a jack hammer against his ribs. The beam caught upon blood-streaked skin, pulling him up short. A cavity in the wall to his left was jammed with body parts. A random assortment of human limbs, wallaby legs and tails were stuffed together in a makeshift larder within the frozen earth. Ahead, two more tunnels branched off, likely heading to the surface.

A metallic chirp echoed through the space. Carter swallowed, his mouth suddenly dry. He shone the torch into the far recesses of the underground vault. At the limit of his light's reach, two multi-faceted eyes shone back.

That's not a bloody dog.

The creature chirped again, the sound vibrating through Carter's chest as it advanced into his torch beam properly. He took an involuntary step backwards, trying to process the impossible information his eyes provided his brain. A freakish beast crept towards him on four limbs, a mix of humanoid and insect features. The body was divided into two segments of thorax and abdomen, all sealed within a dark-brown exoskeleton. Sparse, thick hair sprouted from its legs and back, crowning its scalp like barbed wire. Compound eyes filled the upper two thirds of the creature's face, reflecting Carter's torch like a hundred miniature candles. Pincers erupted from either side of a toothed jaw, drops of venom glistening on their tips as they clicked together.

"Stop there!" ordered Carter. "Or I'll shoot!"

The beast's head tilted to the side as it regarded this intruder to its subterranean home. It stood upright on two spindly legs, mimicking Carter's posture. Its arms were near the same length as the lower limbs, but ended in crude hands, each digit tipped by cruel, hook-like claws. It dragged the female hiker with one hand, her lifeless body limp as a doll. The head lolled unnaturally, a bloody rent where the creature had gnawed at the hiker's neck.

The creature turned its head to the side and chirped again, this time with a different cadence, a mix of short and longer sounds. Scuttling noise sounded from one of the tunnels, followed by answering calls.

Fuck.

Seeing the hiker dead, any need of caution was finished. He didn't need to understand how this beast had come to be. No, he would just treat it like any of the fucked up things he'd survived. There was no understanding how an organisation could send out child suicide bombers and consider it a legitimate tactic of war. And now it was nature throwing him a curveball.

Carter squeezed off a shot, aiming centre of mass as the creature darted to the side. It screamed as the round punched a hole in the left shoulder, but the impact barely slowed its momentum. The beast smashed into him, knocking the gun from his hand and pulling him to the ground. Carter landed on his back, winded, mouth gaping like a fish as he punched at the beast with torch in hand.

Carter's world was reduced to a chaos of moving limbs, saliva, shadows and pain. The beast gripped each of his shoulders with its bony fingers and lunged down at his face, pincers snapping. He jammed the torch under its chin, managing to just keep it at bay as he sought blindly with his other hand for the gun.

Finally he found the Glock's grip, shoved the barrel against the chitinous plates of the beast's armpit and squeezed the trigger twice. Instead of plunging into the beast's heart, the angle was wrong, the rounds blasting upward from armpit to shoulder. The creature screamed and pushed away, oozing an orange mess from the wound. It gripped the mangled trauma of its now useless arm, ripped it off and cast it aside. Chest heaving as he regained his feet, Carter shone his torch at the other tunnels, in time to see two more beasts crawl forth.

They were the Soul Feeders from the Indigenous legends, had to be. Carter fired a hurried round that missed, dirt spurting from the tunnel wall beside one of their heads.

It was enough.

The creatures withdrew, the injured beast chasing after them. Carter's instinct was to follow, but if the next tunnel was as narrow as the first, he would have no room to manoeuvre. A muffled gunshot sounded in the distance and his gut dropped. It could mean only one thing — there was another exit to ground level and his colleague was under attack.

With one last look back at the gruesome larder, Carter grabbed the beast's severed arm as evidence and dived back into the tunnel to crawl for the surface.

CHAPTER SIX

Agent Rylan watched Carter's feet disappear, a snake of nerves coiling in her abdomen. It should have been her in that tunnel. Carter might be ex-special forces, but he'd never come in contact with a cryptid. In her experience, people struggled to process first contact with a creature that shouldn't exist. Rylan's last partner had come with extensive combat experience as well, and yet, when confronted with a shape-shifting cryptid in the abandoned subway tunnels of Sydney, he'd frozen. A moment of indecision that had cost the man his life.

"Martin, I need to scout for another opening like this. If there's something down there, Carter might flush it out another tunnel. Can you help me?" She knew it was a big ask of a civilian, but there was little time.

The ranger nodded, face drawn and pale as he headed further into the bush to the right, scouting the ground at his feet while Rylan headed left. She waded forward, quickly sinking to her thighs in a snow drift. Faint gunshots sounded somewhere deep below, followed by a metallic screech.

Rylan climbed back to firm ground, running back to the tunnel entrance when snow exploded to her right, lifting the ranger clean off the ground. The other entrances to the den must have been covered by snow, used less than the one they'd identified. Three beasts emerged from the hole, standing on hind legs once clear of the tunnel confines. They stood tall, at least seven foot. Thin, bony and menacing, they gave her an uncanny reminder of the trio of stones Martin had pointed out on their way to the hut. The first to emerge had Martin skewered on its forearm, taloned fingers of the beast punching front to back through his abdomen like a spear. It flicked his body aside, the limb sliding from his body with a slurp. Martin hit the ground and curled into a foetal position around his injury, groaning with agony.

"Get away from him!"

One dropped to all fours, ready to charge at her. It emitted a metallic chirp, something vibrating on its back to cause the sound, then it burst into a sprint. A virtual blur, Rylan fired two rounds. The beast skidded to the side and then barrelled into her, knocking her flying. Keeping hold of her pistol, she rolled to her knees, bringing her weapon back to bear. The creature had continued to run after hitting her, passing the hut and streaking into the bush behind. Knowing any further shots would be wasted, she turned her attention back to Martin.

Only one of the beasts remained. Missing an arm, it knelt above the ranger, pointed mandibles spread wide to either side of its mouth. Suddenly it lunged down, puncturing either side of Martin's throat with the pincers. Small sacs behind the mandibles pulsed, injecting massive amounts of venom. The flesh of his neck swelled like a virulent red balloon, before it disengaged.

Rylan fired as she ran, her first round driving into the abdomen of the beast, the second plunging through its neck. She drove a striker's kick into its head, knocking it off the ranger's body. It flipped onto the snow, spattering orange muck as it convulsed, the exoskeleton clacking together as the joints contracted to their maximum range of motion. Rylan jammed the muzzle of her pistol against one of its eyes and squeezed the trigger. Like a puppet with its strings cut, it fell still, finally dead.

Martin's eyes bugged open, mouth gaping as he tried to draw breath. The swelling to his throat was severe, closing his airway like a vice. Rylan knelt at his side and shoved her fist against the abdominal wound to slow the bleeding. It was a futile effort. Martin's face went beet red, then blue with lack of oxygen before mercifully, he lost consciousness. His hands fell away from his throat, body limp. Rylan sought Martin's carotid artery and felt his pulse pass to nothing under her touch.

He was gone. A man that if not for her, wouldn't have come in contact with the creature. She rocked back on her heels, eyes closed for a moment in frustration before standing. There was no time for self-recriminations, the show was just getting started. A sound from the tunnel drew her attention and she spun about, raising her gun.

"Easy, it's just me," said Carter, crawling to his knees.

Rylan lowered her arm, flicking back on the safety as she ran back up the slope. Carter's front was a slick of muddy gore but none of the blood seemed to be coming from an obvious wound. He held an amputated arm by the wrist, coarse spikes of hair bristling from its dorsal surface.

"You okay? Any of that blood yours?"

Carter shook his head. "I'm fine, just a few bruises. I got there too late for the hiker though. It's a fucking charnel house down there, walls stuffed with body parts." He glanced at the limb in his grip before dumping it on the ground with a grimace. "There were three of the bastards; I injured one, but they got away. You have any luck topside when they came out?"

"I killed one while it was attacking the ranger, but the other two are still active."

He glanced sharply up at the mention of the civilian. "Did he make it?" Rylan gave a slight shake of her head in the negative, and Carter spat sourly. "Fuck. Which way did the other two go?"

"One of them shot up the hill, past the hut. Not sure where the second one went, but I think it bolted in the other direction."

"Just a sec," said Carter, looking over his shoulder up the slope. "The cross-country ski trail's up that way, isn't it?"

"Yeah, there's also a downhill ski run," said Rylan, seeing the chairlift above the trees in the distance. As she stared at it, the suspended seats suddenly swung slightly as the chairlift shuddered into life. Rylan pulled up her jacket sleeve to check the time on her watch.

Shit.

Eight fifty-nine AM. She swallowed, spit tacky in her mouth. The cross-country ski race was about to start, along with the opening of the downhill runs. In the distance, a horn sounded, followed by music blaring from speakers along the ski run.

"Is that what I think it is?" asked Carter. "Please tell me it's not that time already?"

Rylan swore. "We need to get the dead creature back to the resort. With this evidence, Freidman won't have a choice but to shut it all down."

"What about the skiers?" said Carter. "We've got two pissed off freaks, soon to be surrounded by a smorgasbord of prey." He drew his Glock and loaded a fresh magazine. "You've seen how those things move, they're natural killers. If we don't take them out, they'll slaughter everything in their path."

"With a handgun?" Rylan shook her head. "It won't be enough. We need the rifles in the gun safe."

"No time." Carter holstered his handgun and picked up the beast's severed arm. "You need to take this back to the resort for Freidman to shut the slopes. I'll tail the creatures and try and hold them off the skiers until then."

Rylan felt anger rise. "I'm not your lackey to order about, Carter. I'm the senior agent on this investigation."

Carter didn't break stride.

"No shit. But, I *am* your bloody team mate, and we're both dealing with the shit hand thrown at us. Doesn't change the fact we need to be in two different locations at once. If you want to take the chase up, it's obviously your call, but I'm shit at politics. You'll have a much better chance at convincing Freidman to act. Your call, boss."

CHAPTER SEVEN

Powdered snow spurted from the back wheels of Agent Rylan's SUV as she left for the Silver-Trust lodge, the cryptid's severed limb safely stowed in the back seat. Carter stared after her for a moment, brow creased against the snow glare before turning the key in the ignition of Martin's Land Rover. He'd had to run his hands through the dead man's blood soaked pockets for the key, feeling like a thief robbing a battlefield corpse.

The engine turned over, grumbling into life with a throaty roar. He spun the wheel, completing a three-point turn to drive further up the mountain in pursuit of the beasts. The vehicle bucked over pot-holes in the fire-trail, tyre chains providing grip on the slippery surface.

Rylan had looked ready to punch him for a minute back at the hut. In hindsight, she would've had plenty of blokes try to push her around in the past. That Rylan had given him leeway on hearing his rationale was a point in her favour—he'd worked with officers who'd rather fail than take advice from a subordinate.

Neither had she backed down during the fight. Rylan had killed a beast single handed, something he couldn't yet claim. She'd proven herself a capable fighter, one that didn't need a burnt-out soldier for protection. When he got back to the lodge, he owed Rylan an apology. He'd made little effort to hide disappointment at his posting to her unit, and initial disbelief in cryptids.

Carter spied the track they'd descended earlier, one that would take him back to the storage shed and cross-country ski trail. Fresh snow shrouded their earlier tyre marks as he turned the wheel and began climbing the steep switchbacks of the trail, engine roaring under the old vehicle's hood. Soon the shed appeared, its straight lines at odds to the surrounding natural landscape. Carter skidded to a stop next to a red flag denoting the cross-country trail. He peered to either side and saw with frustration a skier disappear over the far rise. There was nothing he could do for that competitor, but at least he could stop any more heading into danger.

A freezing breeze trembled the leaves of a snow gum outside his window, sending a shower of snow, fine as icing sugar to the ground. He climbed from the Land Rover, zipping his overcoat to the chin. The bitter cold stung, his cheeks red as capillaries dilated to raise the temperature of the skin and prevent cell damage from the sub-zero conditions. A pair of snow-shoes were on the back seat of the Land Rover and Carter quickly strapped them onto his boots. Unlike the old-school snow-shoes that looked like a pair of massive tennis racquets, the modern version were more like a small, wide pair of skis. With them on his feet, he'd be able to traverse softer sections of snow without sinking.

A black raven erupted from a high branch with a disgusted caw, wings flapping as it gained height. Carter froze, hand reaching for his weapon as he searched for what had startled the bird. On the downward slope of the cross-country trail, another skier came into view. Dressed in a form fitting jacket and leggings emblazoned with the colours of the Belgian flag, the man powered along, using twin poles to help movement. Unlike downhill skis, cross-country skis attach at the toes, allowing the heel to rise with each long stride. Another ten competitors were close on the heels of the Belgian. Carter stepped into the middle of the trail and raised his hand.

"Stop!" he yelled. "The race is cancelled, you need to return to the lodge."

The lead skier ignored him, waving a pole for Carter to get out of his way. The other skiers also paid him no mind, seemingly only intent on catching up with the Belgian.

Carter drew his Glock and fired a shot in the air. "I said *STOP!*"

At the noise of the discharge, he finally got their attention. The competitors skidded to a halt before him.

"What the hell are you doing?" growled the Belgian between heaving breaths.

Carter pulled his badge from his coat pocket, flashing the insignia of his role. "I'm a federal agent. It's no longer safe for you on the mountain, the race is cancelled and you need to return to the hotel."

"Do you know who I am?" said the Belgian.

Oh, for fucks sake.

He didn't have time for this shit. "No, nor do I care," said Carter.

"I am Karl Fischer, gold medallist of the 2018 Winter Olympics." He shoved at the agent with the end of his ski pole, trying to push him aside. "Now, get out of my way."

Carter held his ground, rapidly losing patience. "I can't let you do that, sir."

"Or what?" sneered Karl. "You'll shoot me?" He side stepped out of reach, then skied onward, leaving Carter behind with jaw clenched in anger.

"Hey man, is that blood?" asked one of the remaining competitors.

Carter nodded, opening the front of his thick coat to reveal a slick of gore covering his jumper and trousers. The skier's face paled as he stumbled backward.

"I told you, it's not safe here. You need to return to the lodge. *Now.*"

More competitors were arriving, angry mutters of confusion spreading at the race's suspension.

"Jesus, what the hell is *that?*" said one of the skiers, pointing at the ridge ahead.

Carter spun about. For a second, he saw nothing, before identifying the creature high in a snow gum overhanging the trail. Its brown and grey exoskeleton camouflaged almost perfectly with the bark of the tree, rendering it invisible until it moved. Carter glanced back at the Olympic medallist who laboured up the slope toward it, oblivious of the predator in waiting.

Carter chambered a round in his handgun, wishing like all hell that he had a rifle instead as he glanced back at the small crowd of skiers. "All of you, get the hell out of here. Tell anyone you pass to return to the lodge at once."

Carter started an ungainly run after the Belgian, ski shoes crunching in the icy snow with every step. "Fischer!" he yelled. "Watch out above!" But it was too late.

The beast dropped from the tree, a brown blur as it streaked to the ground, hind feet foremost like a hawk-strike onto a defenceless rabbit. Fischer grunted at the impact, talons puncturing his upper chest as he was smashed onto his back.

Carter wanted to shoot but at this distance was at risk of hitting the skier by accident. He powered on, knowing that he had no chance of making it in time, a growl of fury in his throat.

The creature stooped over its victim, gripped the skier's head by the hair with one hand, the other speared up under the chin. Taloned fingers punctured into the mouth so that it gripped his chin like a handle. Fischer screamed, his agony a garbled wail of blood. The beast stared at Carter, then with a mighty wrench decapitated the poor bastard with the sound of tearing flesh. Blood spurted in a hot arc, pumping from severed carotid arteries. Steam rose from where it landed, turning white to scarlet slush.

Carter skidded to a halt and sighted on the beast. There was no fear of hitting the Belgian now, that ship had sailed. He squeezed off two quick shots as the creature leapt off the corpse, ribs collapsing beneath its feet with a sickening crunch. Bark spurted off a trunk showing his bullet strike, but the creature remained unharmed. He tracked the Soul Feeder, moving so fast between the trees that it was almost a blur. Carter fired one last shot before giving up, knowing he had little ammunition to waste.

Screams sounded from the skiers behind Carter, and he glanced over his shoulder to see the last competitors frantically retreating toward the lodge. He paused, steam billowing in large clouds as he caught his breath. Carter was torn. Should he follow the group down and ensure they returned safely, or chase the beast?

Clenching his jaw, he stared in the direction that the beast had run and saw a chair full of people suspended above the tree-tops, travelling up the mountain. He'd almost forgotten the downhill routes had opened at the same time as the cross-country ski race—and the beast was headed straight for them. Carter tramped off the path into the trees, eyes set on his next destination. The earpiece beeped in his left ear, a call from Rylan. He could only pray she had better news than what he was about to relay.

***

Agent Rylan tapped her foot on the floor, agitation mounting at the delay as she waited outside the hotel morgue. She had created somewhat of a stir in the reception area on her return. Skidding the ute to a halt at the front entrance of the lodge, she had elbowed her way past rich guests to demand an immediate meeting with Freidman. Her dishevelled state and blood-spattered clothes had left the concierge white faced and speechless, nodding dumbly at her request.

That had been five minutes ago. She glanced at her watch, lips thin with frustration. Every second wasted was another potential death, another moment that her new colleague was facing the creatures on his own. She held the wrapped limb as ready proof. One end of the package was soaked in blood, dripping to form a small puddle of orange on the tiles below. Down the hallway, the lift emitted a melodic 'bing' before the doors slid open. The portly Freidman waddled into the hallway, followed closely by his guard.

About fucking time.

The CEO's face was red, shirt collar cutting into his plump neck like a noose. Freidman's eyes narrowed as he caught sight of Rylan and he closed the distance with surprising speed, a finger stabbing at her threateningly.

"Who the fuck do you think you are?" he fumed. "You can't just demand a meeting at the drop of a hat."

Rylan stared at him levelly, her pulse not raising one iota. Self-important bastards like Freidman had little effect on her, aside from the irritation of not being allowed to dish out a swift uppercut to the jaw.

"Close the ski fields and cancel the race," said Rylan, her face stern.

Freidman sneered. "Our deal hasn't changed. I'll do no such thing until I have evidence."

Rylan quickly glanced up and down the hall to ensure they were alone, then flicked aside one side of the jacket wrapped around the beast's limb.

Freidman's eyes bugged. "Jesus, is that—"

"An arm?" said Rylan. She stared down at the freakish limb. Under the lights, the brown exoskeleton revealed fine swirls of different shades, the shell covered in sparse wiry strands of black hair. "It is, but not from any known species." Rylan covered the limb again and gestured at the door to the morgue. "Open it, please."

Still staring at the bundle in her arms, Freidman fished a master key from his pocket and unlocked the door. Agent Rylan strode past him, opened a door upon the body fridge and pulled out an empty stainless-steel trolley to place the limb upon.

"You wanted evidence? You've got it. The owner of this arm is dead, but there's still two more of these creatures loose on the mountain."

Freidman's guard, Ash, squatted next to the trolley to get an eye-level view of the limb. "And I bet they're somewhat pissed off now, eh?"

"Well I don't think they want to kiss and make up," grated Rylan. "It's already killed another two hikers along with a park ranger."

The guard barked a harsh laugh before comparing the length of the arm to his own. "The bastard thing is almost twice the length of mine. How tall was it?"

Rylan closed her eyes for a moment, an image of the beast with its forearm stabbed through the ranger's abdomen in her mind's eye. "At least seven foot tall. They're strong, and can move far more quickly than we can hope to follow on foot. My colleague is in pursuit of one at the moment."

"You have a random body part," said Freidman. Having now composed himself, he leaned against a desk with his arms crossed, expression guarded. “It doesn’t prove it killed my maintenance personnel. If I’m to destroy Silver-Trust’s reputation on its opening day, I want irrefutable proof.”

“Are you fucking nuts?” Rylan raised an eyebrow, caught off guard. “I should remind you, as a federal agent I don’t need your permission to shut this place down. I’m doing you a courtesy and hoping that by working together, the process of coordinating staff and communicating with your patrons will run more smoothly, and *save lives*. But for the sake of argument,” she ripped open the next fridge door, rolled out the first corpse and unzipped the body bag. “Take a look at these wounds, the abdomen might have been cut by a scalpel, while the larger muscles have been precisely excised. You want a smoking gun, then just check out the talons on our friend over there.”

Ash lifted the beast’s hand, spreading the long bony fingers. Three had spiked talons less than an inch long, while the index finger was tipped by a fearsome weapon. A six-inch razor-sharp spike of obsidian extended from its tip.

“She’s not wrong, boss. It carries a ready-made filleting knife,” said Ash.

Freidman huffed. “Okay, but where’s the rest of its body? If I’m going to play ball, I want the entire corpse before some bloody tourist uploads pictures to the internet. If you take Ash to retrieve the body, I’ll close the runs and call off the race.”

Rylan stared at the bodyguard. Most people would appear a little hesitant to engage a monster, but not Ash. He met her appraisal undaunted. Pupils were mildly dilated and he stood with his weight on the balls of his feet, the look of a man ready to launch into action in an instant. The look of a fighter that could handle themselves.

"Are you armed?"

Ash opened one side of his jacket, showing the grip of a 9mm Beretta in a chest holster. "Well enough, love. You won't have to look after me."

"Refer to me as *'love'* again, and I'll gut you myself." Rylan grit her teeth as the bodyguard smirked at her reaction. "The park ranger's body also needs retrieval. I'll take you to the track leading to Rankin's Hut, but outside that, the plan will stay fluid. There's two beasts loose on the mountain, and Agent Carter may require support."

Ash cracked his knuckles and nodded.

Rylan slammed the doors of the body fridge shut and made for the exit. "Meet me out front of reception in two minutes." Without waiting for a response, she started running for the lift, touching her earpiece as she went.

"Agent Carter, shut down of the ski fields is in progress. I'm retrieving rifles and will proceed to your location. Please provide a SITREP. Over."

CHAPTER EIGHT

Carter pushed himself onwards, ignoring the grinding sensation in his hip. Despite the freezing wind, his undershirt was soaked and face a sheen of sweat. He batted aside a hanging branch from his path, releasing a cascade of brilliant white to fall down the neck of his jacket. Carter grimaced as the snow melted on hot skin, sending icy trickles down his back. The natural beauty of the park was at odds to the music pumping from speakers along the ski slopes, sounds that would have been more at home in the hotel bar than up on the mountain.

He glanced upwards. *Not far to go.* The trees ended twenty paces ahead and then he'd be on one of the lodge's blue runs. The music abruptly cut out, and in its absence, Carter heard the harsh sounds of skis cutting through snow for the first time, as the first people of the season descended the slope above.

"Ladies and gentlemen," boomed a deep voice over the speakers. "May I have your attention. Unfortunately, there's been an incident that requires Silver-Trust to close the ski runs today. I request that all people return to the lodge immediately. I repeat, all skiers must return to the lodge immediately. This will hopefully be a temporary measure, and we apologise for the inconvenience."

About fucking time.

The announcement should have been made well before. Suddenly a scream cut the air, high-pitched with terror. A heartbeat later, it was joined by a cacophony of others.

Shit.

Carter pushed himself harder, driving up the last section of bush slope to spill onto the ski run. The screams were coming from downhill and he dropped to a knee, drawing his Glock to search for a target. The Soul Feeder was little over fifty metres away, slicing bloody carnage out of the skiers.

"Shoot it for God's sake! It's killing them all!"

Carter ignored the skier who'd skidded to a halt behind him, and broke into an ungainly run. There was no clear shot, he had to get closer. With the uncoordinated snow shoes on foot, he kept clacking his heels together, nearly sending himself into an ungainly tumble down the slope. The Soul Feeder darted amongst the skiers, powerful legs making impossibly large leaps from one victim to the next.

Steam billowed from Carter's mouth as he saw the beast target a group of four. It knocked a man to the ground as it landed, one foot on his face and the other his chest. It flexed long bony toes, plunging talons deep into the man's cheek and eye. Instead of finishing off the victim below, the creature stabbed out a long arm, skewering a woman through the throat with its six-inch talon. With a deft flick of the wrist, it tore the talon forward, opening the throat from front to back. Blood spurted high, steaming as it hit the snow. Eyes bulging, the woman gripped her neck as if trying to hold her head in place, before slumping to the ground.

The beast changed position on top its first victim, precipitating a gut-turning crunch from the man's neck as his vertebrae fractured. It launched at the other two skiers, catching them as they tried to escape down the slope and slammed into their backs. The three figures tumbled in a flurry of white. The Soul Feeder arose from the mess with a face gripped in each hand. The skiers screamed, hitting at the creature ineffectually before it mashed their heads together, breaking the skulls like eggs. A mush of grey, white and red oozed from the trauma onto the snow as the beast stood to its full height and screamed.

It was no longer killing to feed or stock its larder. The Soul Feeder was in a rage, killing indiscriminately under a berserker blood lust. Carter swerved around a fallen victim, but his left snow-shoe tangled in a loop of intestine, tripping him over. He went with it, landing in prone position with gun extended. The beast was no more than twenty paces away as Carter began to squeeze the trigger. The person his foot was tangled within groaned and kicked out, knocking Carter's aim off as the gun fired.

The Soul Feeder stumbled backwards a step, a hand raised to its head. The pincers either side of its jaw clenched repeatedly, venom oozing in a slow trickle from their ends as it screamed. His round had creased the exoskeleton of its skull, drilling a runnel along the side of its head. Carter squeezed the trigger again, heart dropping as the hammer clicked on an empty chamber.

Fuck.

He slapped a hand to his waist, fumbling to raise his jacket and access the underlying ammunition pouch. The Soul Feeder roared again, expressionless eyes staring straight at Carter as it leapt toward him with forearms outstretched like a freakish praying mantis. Carter lost grip of the magazine as he rolled to the side. The creature mashed into the snow, feet missing his torso by a hand's breadth.

Carter stared up as it bent over him, breath tight in his chest as he madly tried to load his last magazine. The Soul Feeder backhanded him with the force of a baseball bat, smashing the gun from his grip. Carter scrabbled after it, but the creature gripped the hood of his jacket and ripped him backwards, throwing him ten paces down the slope as if no more than a bundle of rags. The Soul Feeder picked up the gun and paused, turning the implement this way and that, as if trying to work out how to use the weapon. With a finger looped through the trigger guard it turned the barrel towards itself, staring into the eye of darkness at the end.

Do me a favour and shoot yourself.

With a guttural sound, it tossed the gun into the trees before looking back at Carter, glittering eyes staring with the intensity of a cobra. The agent pulled himself to his feet, arms out slightly from his side as he glanced about for something, anything to use as a weapon.

"Hey, you freak! Leave him alone!" yelled a man from above.

Carter glanced up to see a man in his mid-fifties on the chairlift, an open beer can in one hand while he shook a ski pole threateningly with the other. The chair hung immobile just short of a supporting tower, brought to a stop at the announcement of the run closure moments before.

Ah, shit. Don't draw its attention. Carter raised a finger to his lips, eyes pleading for the man to be quiet.

"Don't worry, mate. It won't get me up here, I've got your back."

The man leaned over his guard rail and threw one of his ski poles at the Soul Feeder. The implement cartwheeled through the air before striking the creature point first. The spike lodged between the plates of burnished exoskeleton at its left shoulder.

The beast screeched in pain, wrenched the spike from its body and tossed it aside as it looked up at its attacker.

"Hell yeah, take that you prick!" shouted the man.

The Soul Feeder stretched to full height, arms spread wide. Blood trickled from its shoulder, a slick of scarlet over the plates of its chest. Suddenly it drew its arms together, and with a creaking sound, two wings burst from beneath plates on its back. They unfolded, doubling in length, each partially transparent with a golden shimmer to their surface. The man on the chairlift blanched, then threw his remaining pole at the beast, followed by his can of beer.

The Soul Feeder leapt into the air and the wings buzzed into motion, a blur of movement. It seemed unsure in the air, clumsy and slow compared to its movement on the ground. Each of the suspended chairs were at capacity, three or four people to a bench. Screams broke out along the line, cries for help as the beast ascended. One man farther up the hill kicked off his skis and jumped for the pole beside his chair. The icy metal slipped through his grip and he plummeted ten metres to hit the concrete block at its base with a dull thud.

Carter waved his arms and yelled himself hoarse. "Come on, you bitch! I'm the one who creased your fucking skull. Face me instead!"

The Soul Feeder ignored him and circled up the tower before grabbing a foot of the man who'd thrown the pole. He kicked out, struggling to escape its grip, a garbled cry of fear on his lips. With a vicious tug, the creature ripped him out from beneath the guard rail, the extra weight causing the beast to dip in the air as the man struggled upside down. It swung him to the right, smacking his skull cruelly against the steel tower pole before dropping the limp body. Hovering in the air, it turned and looked for a new target.

Uninjured guests on the slope took their chance, skiing for the lodge and safety. Within moments, those on the chairlift were the only prey available. The Soul Feeder ripped a woman off a seat and flicked a talon across her throat, silencing her scream. Carter couldn't do anything from the ground, not without a weapon. He pressed the ear piece hooked over his left ear.

"Rylan? I have one active cryptid and multiple casualties on the ski run. I need one of the rifles, ASAP. Over." He paused, waiting for a reply. Nothing.

Fuck, where the hell are you?

He'd heard nothing from her since leaving the cross-country track. At that stage, she'd been preparing to leave the lodge again, rifles in hand. And now with ongoing radio silence, he was concerned she'd been attacked by the second Soul Feeder.

"Rylan, what's your situation? Over."

Still nothing. Carter grimaced and turned his attention back to the screaming tourists above. Without a gun, he was left with no choice. He'd have to bring the fight to the Soul Feeder.

Carter ran to the closest support pole and kicked off his snow shoes. On the shoe's sole was a spike-toothed crampon for grip in the snow and ice. Made of jagged steel, it looked like a single side of a bear trap. He ripped the attachment free, then set his foot on the first rung of a metal ladder to climb the pole. Freezing air whipped about his shoulders, a grim contrast to warm blood spattering his face from a new victim above. Carter clenched his teeth and started to climb.

CHAPTER NINE

Rylan gunned the ute's engine up the steep track, tyre-chains providing just enough traction to keep her from sliding off the edges. She was pushing her luck, but every second of delay left Agent Carter with only a handgun to protect himself and others. The turn-off to Rankin's Hut approached on the right, but she kept the wheels straight.

"Hey, aren't you taking that exit?" asked Ash.

She shook her head. "My priority's to keep your patrons and my partner alive. I'll take you there afterwards."

"Bullshit." Ash pulled a Beretta from inside his jacket and jabbed the barrel into her chest. "I don't give a shit about your priorities. I want that creature's body. Now."

Rylan glanced down at his gun, eyes flint-hard as they flicked back up to his face. "This better be a joke."

Ash chambered a round, a half-smile on his lips. "Nope."

For fucks sake.

Rylan did as instructed and pulled into the turn-off. The road was a dead-end, terminating in a small car park where the walking track commenced. Keeping the gun trained on her, Ash climbed out of the cabin.

"Leave your weapon on the passenger seat and get me one of those rifles."

Teeth grinding hard enough to snap, Rylan placed her handgun on the seat before handing Ash one of the M4 Carbines.

"Follow that track until you reach the hut. You'll find the bodies twenty paces down the slope, south of the building." Rylan was itching to string the bastard up, but getting stuck in a fight here would cost civilian lives.

"You can show me when we get there. You're coming along for the ride."

"Enough!" she growled, climbing out of the driver's seat to stab a finger in his chest. "You're impeding an investigation and putting more lives at risk, not to mention threatening a federal agent. I'll see you in prison for the next two decades!"

Ash took a half-step backward, surprised by her sudden movement. "Watch it, bitch. I'm the one holding the rifle."

"What are you going to do, shoot me?" Rylan sneered. "What's so important about this cryptid to you and Freidman that you'd risk criminal charges?" She stared at the bodyguard, saw the twitch of his eyelid, knew he was holding something back. And then it hit her, a light bulb flicking on in her brain.

"Silver-Trust Pharmaceutical's invested significant capital into senolytics over the past decade without success?" Rylan saw the bodyguard's expression harden and knew she was on the right track. "Drugs that work to slow down the aging process, the new fucking fountain of youth." Rylan paused, shaking her head that she hadn't seen this coming earlier. "Freidman wants to study how this creature's achieved such longevity, doesn't he? I bet the prick thinks he can convert it to a breakthrough in senolytic research. Silver-Trust is huge already, but can you imagine how much money would be generated by a drug that enabled you to live for centuries?"

Ash dropped the rifle to hang by its sling, face hard as he calmly drew a combat knife from his belt. "That's a theory Freidman would prefer you kept to yourself. Word travels fast these days, Agent Rylan. If our competitors found out, we'd be fighting off constant cyber-attacks to steal the information."

Ash's hand blurred into motion, stabbing the blade forward. Caught off guard by his sudden attack, Rylan's attempt to block his strike failed. The knife sliced her jacket like parchment, piercing her belly and driving up under the ribs into a lung. Agony bloomed, the muscles of her abdominal wall spasming about the blade. Ash callously twisted the blade and ripped it free.

Crimson flecked Rylan's lips as her mouth gaped, unable to draw breath. She drove a fist against the wound to slow the haemorrhage and collapsed to her knees, her vision already greying at the edges.

I don't have time for this…

"A gunshot wound would be hard to ignore, but a stab wound?" Ash stared down at her with a face absent of emotion, his dark eyes soulless as a shark. "Well, that could be blamed on these sadistic beasts you're chasing. Time for you to stop making my life difficult." He reversed the knife in his grip and slashed it across the front of her throat, opening it ear to ear.

Rylan slumped to the ground, blood pumping hot and red into the snow as the world went black.

***

Ash left her body where it fell. The less of his DNA on her body, the better. He was majorly pissed. Killing the agent hadn't been part of his plan, but he knew Freidman wouldn't tolerate his secret being exposed. Better to get the job done now before she had a chance to tell the other agent.

Ash pulled a body-bag from the tray of the ute and shoved it along with a few mags of ammunition into his backpack. He wasn't looking forward to dragging the creature back by himself, but shrugged off his annoyance. If one of the beasts sniffed out his trail, hauling a dead weight over rough terrain would be the least of his worries.

After completing a quick weapons check and chambering a round, Ash set off for Rankin's Hut at a jog.

***

Rylan's eyes opened suddenly, lungs sucking in a deep breath. She groaned and rolled to her back, touching a hand to her throat. Although the flesh had healed, she still felt the blade's edge with the sharpness of a burn. Her gut was little better, but she grit her teeth and climbed to her feet. The pain would ease over the next hour, pink scars fading quickly until imperceivable. During the previous three hundred years of her life, Rylan had suffered far worse injuries and risen to fight again.

Ash was nowhere to be seen and she needed to get moving and make contact with Carter. Rylan's ear-set had torn free during the attack. Turning on the spot, she found it submerged in bloody slush and swore as she picked it up. Soaked with water, the device was ruined.

Gunshots sounded in the distance. Rylan's head snapped toward their origin, the same direction Carter had said he was headed for the cross-country track. Rylan might have lost radio contact, but at least she knew where to find her partner. She climbed back in the ute, slammed the door and revved the engine to life.

***

Ash buried the hatchet into the Soul Feeder's hip with a dull *thunk*. Finding the soft tissue between exoskeleton plates, the blade sliced deep, almost to the snow beneath. He levered the blade sideways and the remaining tendrils of muscle and sinew ripped like fabric. Ash tossed the hatchet aside, picked up the leg and began stuffing it into the body bag with the other severed parts. The creature had been too tall to fit without some structural modification.

A loud trill echoed from a patch of snow gums farther down the slope. It was a weird noise he couldn't quite place, like an insect through a metal synthesizer. If it'd been in the middle of summer, he probably wouldn't have paid attention, but in the dead of winter, the misplaced noise was unsettling. During the past hour, the frequency of calls had intensified, following him from Rylan's discarded corpse all the way to the hut.

Ash stuffed the last body part into the bag and zipped up the blue plastic. He stood tall and wiped his bloody hands on his jacket, leg muscles and back aching after working in a crouched position. The ranger's face stared at him accusingly, dry eyes seeming to follow his every movement.

"Chill out, old man," said Ash, chuckling. "Ain't like you're going to bloat and rot in this heat. I'll come back for you tomorrow."

Even if he'd wanted to, there was no way he'd be able to return with both corpses. By the time he dragged the creature back to the ute, he was going to be knackered. That, and it would be nearing dark with two cryptids still on the loose.

Something down the slope caught his eye. He turned toward it, searching the undergrowth for further movement. Suddenly, a mound of snow at the base of a tree swelled up before collapsing down again. A dull scraping sound, like nails across rock, emanated from the spot. Ash grabbed hold of the M4 rifle and raised it to his hip, safety off.

The snow bulged upward again, this time a clawed leg breaking through the surface. Another limb punched its way to sunlight, then an insectoid head burst into view between the forelegs. Different to the Soul Feeder he'd dismembered, this creature was dull brown with two red eyes protruding from either side of its head. The beast paused for a moment as if tasting the air, then hauled itself above ground.

What the fuck are you?

Goosebumps puckered along Ash's arms as he watched the abomination start to climb an adjacent tree. The size of a large mastiff, its bloated body was wide with a rubbery exoskeleton, reminding Ash of a dragonfly nymph blown to gargantuan proportions. Either oblivious or uncaring of his presence, it slowly crawled up the trunk, claws leaving deep sap-oozing punctures in the bark until it was roughly four metres off the ground. The nymph dug its claws deep into the wood as the head flexed down to the bark, then became deathly still. Suddenly the spine of the creature bulged upward, a split tearing from neck to the end of its body. Ash swallowed, mouth dry as he glanced at the blue bag at his feet, realising he was watching a juvenile Soul Feeder transform into adult form.

"No you fuckin' don't, not while I'm watching."

Ash raised his weapon and fired a three shot burst, destroying the nymph's head in a welter of orange slime. The body slumped, hanging from two hooked claws for a moment before dropping to the ground. Ash jogged over, leaving deep footprints in the snow until he reached the corpse. Through the split in the nymph's back, he could see a familiar pattern of the adult Soul

Feeder exoskeleton. He stared up into the expanse of tree branches above, searching for other abandoned nymph casings. Now that he knew what to look for, what had passed at a distance as deformities of the branch were anything but. Perfectly camouflaged to the underlying bark, he picked out three empty casings above and another four in the next tree.

Shit. He needed to get out of there.

Ash grasped a leg of the dead nymph, dragged it up to the dismembered adult and shoved it into the body bag. Despite its size, both corpses were lighter than expected, a piece of luck he hadn't expected considering he would need to drag the bag over a kilometre back to the ute. He glanced into the setting sun and zipped up his jacket. The temperature had dropped over the past half hour, a freezing breeze chasing increasingly dark clouds across the sky. Fresh snow was coming, he could taste it on the wind.

A metallic chirp sounded, and this one was louder. Closer. He took hold of the M4 again, finger hovering over the trigger guard as he scanned the closest trees. Leaves shivered, wind raising a mournful howl between the branches. Hair rose on the back of his neck as movement against a trunk caught his eye. An adult Soul Feeder stared down at him, body pressed to the wood like a stick insect. The exoskeleton appeared wet and soft, not yet hardened and stiff like the one in the bag. A freshly exited nymph shell clung to the branch beside it.

Two humps rose from the ground, bulbous nymph heads breaching the mantle of snow a moment later. The newly hatched Soul Feeder stared down at its siblings, emitting another trill, almost of encouragement? In answer, the low noise of scratching increased, and suddenly nymph heads were erupting at the base of snow gums across the slope.

Ash took quick aim and punched a round through the freshly hatched Soul Feeder, then swung the rifle over his shoulder by the sling and grabbed the body bag. He'd seen what one of these creatures could do to a human, and had no desire to be around when this mob was ready to feed.

***

Ash dumped the bag and dropped to a knee, chest heaving and limbs trembling with exhaustion as he lifted the rifle. The beasts hadn't taken long to catch up. They'd trailed at a distance initially, but grown in confidence quickly. A trill sounded again, the sound smacking against his chest like a physical force. Ash scanned right and saw a beast drop from a tree, landing with the grace of a leopard. Acting on instinct he fired twice, one shot in the head, another in its torso.

Another Soul Feeder darted from cover on the left side of the track. Ash's first two shots missed, the third catching an upper leg. The round fragmented on impact, smashing the exoskeleton of the limb like egg shell. In a heartbeat Ash was on his feet, his next two shots turning the Soul Feeder's head to a mulch of brain and blood.

He grabbed the body bag and dragged it up the last thirty metres of slope to the track's car park.

Shit.

The ute was missing and the woman gone, a blood-stained imprint the only evidence left of his crime. Agent Carter must have found and retrieved her body. Ash would soon find out if the ASIO douche had taken the bait and attributed her death to a Soul Feeder attack.

Ash grimaced in irritation as he drew his radio to call the lodge for transport. With more of the freakish beasts closing in behind, he had no desire to stay on the mountain longer than necessary.

CHAPTER TEN

Carter glanced up to see the chairlift jerk into reverse, finally starting to return those stranded skiers upon it to the lodge. The beast continued its rampage; stabbing, cutting and ripping people from their seats. Having flown to the top of the mountain, it was working its way down chair by chair, turning the snow below into an abstract artwork of spattered red and white.

Carter tried to block out the screams of the wounded, focusing on each grip as he climbed the narrow ladder at speed. The metal rungs were slippery, providing little more than a toe hold for his boots. Wind buffeted his body, curling about the exposed skin of his neck with an icy caress, stealing warmth and numbing his fingers. He finally reached the top of the pole. Four-seater chairs passed in opposite directions to either side of him. He reached out an arm to the closest one, however it fell agonizingly short, just shy of his fingertips. Carter would have to jump. But one slip, and he'd plummet twenty metres to a life-ending crunch.

The beast was on the chair coming toward him, insectoid jaws buried in a man's neck. A woman on the next seat along the cable slipped beneath the safety bar, tears streaming down her cheeks as she jumped rather than be eaten alive. An image of the Twin Tower bombings flashed through his brain; office workers leaping to certain death, preferring an end of their own choice than the agonizing one at hand. Carter had to stop it. If he failed, the beast would continue down the line, tearing through hundreds of seats packed with innocent civilians. His heart raced, breath tight in his chest.

Adrenaline surged through his body, providing new energy.

Do it.

Carter jumped, eyes fixed on his target. His hands slapped onto the backrest, feet hanging in free air. The chair swung with his impact, causing his right grip to slip. Carter grunted with effort, hip grinding as he hooked a leg over the armrest and dragged himself onto the seat. The Soul Feeder was at the far end of the bench, long limbs clutching the outside of the structure like a huntsman spider. At Carter's arrival, it withdrew its jaws from the man's neck and screamed at him. Hot blood and spit flecked Carter's cheeks, and he found himself roaring back, a wordless battle cry of terror and fury.

Carter pulled the toothed crampon from his jacket pocket, and with the ungainly piece of metal in hand, Carter knew he was in a fight he couldn't win. He might as well have been holding a toothpick for all the good it would do him. But if it bought time for a few more people to escape, it had to be worth something.

The Soul Feeder tore the lifeless body of its victim beneath the rail and let it drop, then climbed over the edge of the seat. Multifaceted eyes glittered under the sun, reflecting the blue sky and snow in a million tiny images back at the agent. Carter swallowed, knowing he would have one chance only. As the beast crawled within striking distance, the agent lunged forward, stabbing the metal teeth of the crampon at the right eye. The spikes penetrated, tearing the surface like bloody plastic, opening a gooey rent. It roared with agony. A forelimb slapped the implement from Carter's hand before punching him hard in the centre of the chest.

Winded, Carter hit the far side of the seat, nearly falling over the railing. Struggling to draw breath, he felt as if his ribs had been caved in. The beast crouched over him. Blood-stained jelly oozed from its decimated eye as it drew back its hand, the six-inch talon extended.

Suddenly the Soul Feeder's hand exploded as a gunshot echoed off the mountains around. As if surprised, the creature held the stump in front of its face. Carter glanced through the slats of the backrest back up the mountain.

Fuck, yes!

Agent Rylan looked through her rifle sights, using the hood of the ute to steady her aim. She fired a second time, this round catching the beast in the head. A small hole appeared on the near side before punching out a fist-sized exit wound. The Soul Feeder collapsed, exoskeleton clattering against the metal bars before slipping to the ground below.

Carter exhaled a shaky breath and forced himself to sit. With no other way off, he'd have to ride the gore-covered chair back to the lodge. He gave Rylan a wave of thanks, and pointed to the base of the valley to meet her there. Rylan gave him a tired thumbs up, then climbed back behind the steering wheel.

Carter closed his eyes and concentrated on slowing his breathing, taking the chance to rest. Two beasts down, one to go.

CHAPTER ELEVEN

While the reception staff set up the tables he'd requested, Carter turned to address the crowd gathered in the hotel atrium. On exiting the ski lift, he'd immediately demanded the concierge activate the hotel's emergency evacuation siren. All guests of the hotel now thronged the huge ground-floor room, spilling back into the hallways behind. Standing inwhatever they'd been wearing when the alarm sounded, the occasional unlucky person in pyjamas or bathrobe were dotted amongst the crowd of ski jackets and waterproof pants.

The evacuation alarm boomed from speakers on the ceiling, beeping and wailing at ear-splitting volume over the shouting crowd. Carter caught the eyes of the concierge again and pointed at a speaker, then drew a line across his throat. Thankfully, the man understood his meaning and within a few moments the siren cut out. As if to fill the dip in volume, the crowd grew louder again, a hundred questions shouted at him from every corner of the room. Carter thrust a hand in the air for attention.

"QUIET!" he shouted in a voice used to being heard over the noise of a battlefield.

The room quickly fell to a murmur of the preceding chaos. His eyes roamed over the crowd. Some people were tearful, others angry and many just plain confused. Carter ground his teeth together, his jaw aching as the weight of responsibility sunk in. He knew there to be at least one more Soul Feeder alive and if it broke into the lodge, the slaughter would be monumental.

"My name is Agent Eoin Carter, and I work for the Australian Security Intelligence Organisation, what most of you would know as ASIO." He paused for a second, glaring at a talking person until they shut up again. "I want you to *all* listen very carefully. There is little time, and I will not be repeating myself. A group of masked assailants has attacked innocent people on the ski-slopes, killing multiple men and women. Unfortunately, a member of their group is still at large, placing patrons of the Silver-Trust Ski Lodge at unacceptable risk. Under domestic terrorism legislation, I have the legal power to evacuate this entire facility, and will be doing so immediately to ensure everyone's safety."

Carter pointed to the front of the lobby, where hotel staff had set up the four tables he'd requested.

"All must proceed to those tables to submit your name, and surrender mobile phones and electronic devices with photographic capability. Although they will be returned in due course, all devices must first be scanned for photographic evidence that may help identify the killers responsible.

"Next, proceed directly to the train terminal. From there, you will be transported to the function centre at the base of the mountain. Please complete these actions with a minimum of fuss. As I said, there is still one gunman on the loose."

At this, volume quickly escalated once again, some people quickly pushing forward to access the checkpoint.

"Hey!" shouted a man in the middle of the room, waving his arm for Carter's attention. "People have said it's some sort of monster killing people. A giant bug or something?"

Carter pulled a face of dismissive scorn. "Don't be ridiculous, sir. There's no such thing as monsters. The murderer is a freak in a costume. Such outfits are designed as a means to generate additional fear, nothing more."

"But I heard it flew between chairs on the lift? How is that possible?"

A furrow carved between Carter's brows. "They were mistaken, stress can affect memories, sir."

What had his instructor in the agent cadet program said? *'Deny, deny, deny. Until command has agreed upon an official story, the first line of response is always to deny.'*

"A number of patrons were tragically attacked on exiting the ski lift at the top, but there were no wings, no flying bugs. Am I understood?" The man wilted under the intensity of Carter's glare, eventually looking away. "Good. If there are no more questions, please proceed to the tables and commence the evacuation."

A hand gripped his shoulder, fingers digging uncomfortably into his collar bone. He looked down to find Freidman glaring up at him. "What do you think you're doing?"

"You've got ears, sir," said Carter. "And heard just as well as everyone else. The situation has changed since we last met. Your resort is being evacuated. For your own safety, I request you leave with your patrons."

"Like fuck I will, you piece of—"

"You *will* evacuate," said Carter, pulling out a set of flex-cuffs from his jacket. "Or I'll arrest you for obstructing a federal agent. The time for pleasantries are over. Get in the way of me doing my job, and you'll be facing court. Understood?"

Freidman pursed his lips but remained silent, an artery on his forehead pulsing with dangerous pressure. Eventually he turned on the spot and marched away. Carter let out a slow breath, happy to see the back of the man. Why was it that the super-rich always seemed to think there was a different rule for them compared to everyone else?

"Carter."

He turned around, and saw Rylan walking through the door from the car park. Carter paced toward her, meeting her halfway through the lobby where he passed her a replacement Glock pistol she'd requested over the radio. She nodded in thanks, completed a quick weapons check then unzipped her jacket to access her holster.

"Jesus, what happened to your neck?" asked Carter. A thick, red scar puckered the skin above her thyroid cartilage, extending from one ear to the other.

Rylan avoided eye contact, instead, watched Freidman disappear out a side door with a frown on her face. "It's nothing. I had a turtle neck jumper on earlier, must have been tight enough to leave a mark." She zipped her jacket back up to the chin, covering the mark in the process.

Carter let it drop. If she didn't want to talk about, so be it. Wouldn't be the first person to be self-conscious of their scars, although he could have sworn it wasn't there earlier.

"The first train should be ready to leave in thirty minutes. Three return trips will see all patrons evacuated to the mountain base."

"And photographic evidence. Did you get their phones?"

Carter nodded. "Inevitable that some people will have posted photos already, but I'm confiscating all devices at the checkpoint." He pointed at a large box near the lobby doors where a clerk was depositing an expensive iPhone with a tag attached. "I said they'd be returned eventually?"

"Possibly," said Rylan with a slight shrug. "I wouldn't feel bad about it though. These people blow more money on a lunchtime drinks tab than it costs for the latest smartphone." She looked out a window to the ill-fated chairlift. "Besides, after what happened up there, I think most will just be happy to have made it out alive."

Carter swallowed, pushing aside the thought of how close he'd come to death himself. If Rylan had turned up a few seconds later —

Shut up and focus.

"We sighted three of the creatures at Rankin's Hut. With two confirmed kills, that leaves just one on the loose. How do you want to take it from here? Go on the attack, or let it come to us?"

"We can't afford more civilian deaths. Until this place is empty, we're stuck fighting on its own turf."

Carter gave a stiff nod of agreement. "We need feet on the mountain, something to keep attention away from the evacuation operation. Any chance of back-up?"

Rylan shook her head. "I've asked, but at best they're six hours away. Some bullshit happened with the helicopters at our disposal, so they're coming by road."

Carter knew he shouldn't be surprised. The government had been sucking funds from ASIO for the better part of a decade. He paused, biting his bottom lip. "Another set of hands would give us a better chance of success. Maybe we should scope out if Freidman's guard, Ash, will be willing to lend support?"

"No."

"I'm not overjoyed at the prospect either, but the man has battle experience. I can ignore his arrogance if it means keeping our necks intact."

Rylan grimaced, looked over her shoulder and then moved closer to Carter, dropping her voice. "We can't trust Freidman or Ash. They're trying to steal cryptid bodies for the pharmaceutical arm of the Silver-Trust empire. I can't allow this to happen. The carcasses must be returned to our own vetted scientists, people who've signed non-disclosure agreements."

"So, we keep tight control of the cryptids after they're dead. I don't see the issue here," said Carter.

"Ash can't be trusted. He caught me by surprise, attacked me and stole one of the rifles. Because of him, I almost didn't reach you in time." She paused, one hand rubbing at a spot under her ribs. "He placed our lives in danger and I'm going to bloody charge him for it. Next time I see the prick, I'll be cuffing him."

Carter glanced through the reception doors over her shoulder, and saw a twin-cab Silver-Trust ute heading for the underground car park. "Well, looks like you'll get your chance."

Rylan turned, her mouth hardening as she followed his line of sight. She lifted her jacket and drew the Glock. "Let's make this quick. We've got more important shit than this arsehole to deal with."

***

Rylan mentally kicked herself for allowing Carter to see her neck prior to the wound completely healing. She'd fucked up today. Allowing herself to be provoked by Freidman's attack dog had almost cost Carter's life. You'd think after all these years, she'd have learnt to let insults roll off like water, and yet, in some ways it had become harder. Three hundred years she'd been walking the earth, and men still talked to her as if she was a child. And yet, she hadn't thought Ash would resort to violence so quickly. In reflection, she knew he'd weighed the risks and decided her death could be blamed on the beast—an easy solution that only a psychopath would consider, let alone act upon. The man was a loose cannon.

"Stay behind and follow my lead."

Rylan eased off the safety on her handgun and glanced to check on her partner. Carter already had his weapon in hand, face impassive as he walked calmly behind her. About to enter a potentially violent situation, and he looked as if he was about to read the morning paper. She'd seen faces like it before, knew her own in the mirror was one of them. The carefully managed exterior of a person used to shutting down emotion and ignoring their own fear until the job was done. When potential death became part of your everyday life, there was no other way to function.

In the normal world, the skill was a double-edged sword. Relationships suffered for it. When a fight arose, it was easy to bring the shutters down, fall back into a practiced habit to spare the mind more hurt. Previous lovers had called her cold-hearted, unfeeling. By the time they came out with shit like that, she knew the relationship had run its course. Rylan had survived this long with her sanity intact by doing what was needed, and there was no way she'd change for anyone now.

Fuck 'em.

Wait until they'd lived a few centuries and, see how they viewed the importance of something as fleeting as a love affair. She'd learnt the hard way there was no point committing to a long term relationship. Rylan had done it just the once before vowing never to repeat the error. Time had withered her husband's body while leaving her in eternal youth, a disparity that couldn't be ignored forever. At first, he'd been proud of her timeless beauty, but that had inevitably changed. Friends and neighbours alike had begun to whisper of witchcraft. After all, how else could a woman who was supposed to be in her sixties remain so youthful? Seeing the adoring eyes of her husband turn cold and fearful had broken something inside. Knowing there was no way to repair the situation, she'd left before a mob came with a charge of witchcraft on their lips.

As a single woman in the early 1700s, there were few options to earn a living outside a brothel. And so, she'd chosen a different horror. Shaving her hair and binding her breasts, Rylan disguised herself as male to enter the military and escape. Amongst the slaughter of old battlefields, it had been relatively easy to move from unit to unit, and from one theatre of war to another without people noting her longevity. Her current role within ASIO was her first step outside the military in a very long time.

Rylan shook her head slightly and forced her mind back to the job.

The entrance to the morgue was a few paces away, door hanging half open. A smear of orange tracked from the car park lift down the hall, up and through the door ahead. A grunt sounded from within the room, followed by a dull thump as something was dropped. Trusting Carter would be on her heel, she stepped through the doorway with gun raised.

"Hands where I can see them!"

Ash leant over a steel trolley, a large body bag covering its surface. Orange blood oozed from the bag's seams, dripping in slow plops to the ground below. At her voice, the guard froze. Ash held his arms out to the side, his face blanching as he looked up.

"What's the matter, Ash? You look like you've seen a ghost," said Rylan, a smile kinking one corner of her mouth. Carter padded around her, retrieving the M4 from the bodyguard before systematically patting him down for other weapons. Carter ripped Ash's hands behind his back and fastened them with a pair of black zip-cuffs. Satisfied, he backed away.

Ash's gaze flicked between the two of them before centring on Rylan again, his lips parted in confusion. "I thought you were…"

"Dead?" Rylan barked a humourless laugh as she glanced at Carter. "Would you believe this prick tried to stab me in the guts?"

"I didn't just try. I slit your bloody throat, watched you bleed out." He looked at Carter, his face bewildered. "What the fuck's going on? Has this bitch got a twin or something?"

"Hardly." Rylan angled her body away from Carter and unzipped the top of her jacket, exposing the skin of her newly healed neck. "You think I'd be standing here if you'd cut my throat? I was wearing a vest, the knife didn't even penetrate. All you did was wind me." Rylan holstered her gun, taking satisfaction at the self-doubt on his face. "But just because you're incompetent, doesn't mean you get to walk away. I'm charging you with attempted murder, along with theft of evidence from a federal case. The next time you walk free, you'll be a broken old man."

"I'm not crazy, I know what I saw." The bodyguard glared at her, an artery over his temple pulsing like it was about to burst. Lips parted, he looked ready to speak again when his radio crackled to life.

"Ash, are you there? There's been an incident on the course."

The bodyguard glanced at it, lip curled in a sneer. "It's the comms clerk for the resort. I'm somewhat indisposed, so are one of you heroes going to answer that?"

Rylan unclipped the radio from his jacket and pressed the receiver. "This is Agent Rylan speaking. What's happened? Over."

There was a pause on the other end for a moment, before the clerk spoke again. "Ah... Okay. We've received a call from Storage Hut Three on the cross-country ski course. There's a competitor who says he's under attack."

Fuck.

"Can you patch me through?"

"Yeah. Two seconds... right, you're on line with him now."

A metallic clang echoed over the radio, like a sledgehammer smashing into metal sheeting, followed by a panicked yell.

"Hello, sir? This is Agent Rylan speaking. Who am I talking to?"

"This... this is Arvid Olsen." The man sounded close to tears, voice strained. "I need help, there are *demons* trying to break into the hut. I don't know how long this door will hold."

"Sir, you're saying there is more than one creature?"

"Five, ten? I didn't have time to count when they were chasing me!" shouted the man. "I just need *help*. Is someone coming or not?"

"Hold tight, sir. We'll be with you as soon as possible." Rylan cut off the call and looked at her partner.

"I thought there was only one of the bastards left?"

"There can't be any more than that," said Carter. "We've killed two of them already, maybe he's confused?"

"He's not fucking confused," muttered Ash. "Terrified maybe, but not confused."

"What do you mean?" said Rylan.

"When I collected the corpse, I saw more of the freaks crawling from the earth. Not from a tunnel, but directly out of the soil. They were different to the first one." He nodded his head at the bag on the table. "If you don't believe me, take a look in there. I killed one when it started to shed its skin."

Carter holstered his gun, stepped up to the steel trolley and unzipped the body bag. He spread the opening wide, exposing an abattoir of severed body parts. The base of the bag swam with blood in various stages of coagulation.

"Couldn't fit the bastard in, so had to chop it into smaller pieces for transport. The small one's whole though," said Ash.

"Jesus. Rylan, you got to see this," said Carter, his brows drawn together in a frown.

She stepped closer and looked over Carter's shoulder. Spread across the severed pieces of the adult was a creature roughly the size of a German Shepherd. Like a cicada nymph grown to impossible proportions, a split ran along the length of its rubbery brown back, exposing an underlying shell with a similar pattern to the Soul Feeders.

"I spotted a bunch of empty insect casings like that one in the trees up there. Fuck knows how many of the bastards are on the mountain," said Ash.

Rylan rocked back on her heels, mind racing as pieces of the puzzle slotted into place. "We were wrong. These creatures aren't hundreds of years old, they're just the next phase of a life cycle."

"Wouldn't be the first bug to spend time underground before emerging," said Carter. "Cicadas spend around seven years in the nymph stage before emerging and shedding their skin for the final part of life."

"Thankfully these big bastards spend at least thirty years out of the light. But if they're underground for that long, they'd have to be feeding on organic material. What's with the larder of meat you saw in the burrow?"

"First meal for the new hatchlings? A boost of protein to give them strength until they can find their own sustenance, I reckon," said Carter.

"Shit, there could be a swarm of the bastards up there." Rylan pulled a map of the mountain trails from her pocket and turned back to the bodyguard. "The clerk said the emergency call came from Storage Hut Three. Can you point out its location?"

Ash's lips tightened for a second before releasing his breath in a sigh. "Top right of the map. Follow the eastern fire-trail until it connects with the cross-country run."

Carter took the map and spread it on a bench, tracing the bodyguard's directions with his finger until he located the hut. He grabbed a pen off the bench and drew a large cross over the location.

"Right, let's get going," said Carter as he folded up the map.

"Take me with you," said Ash. "I know those trails like the back of my hand. I'll get us there and back in half the time."

"And trust you again? No chance," said Rylan, unconsciously rubbing at a residual ache in the top of her abdomen as she made for the door behind Carter.

"For fucks sake," growled Ash. "Any fool could see I'm no threat to you now. I've seen what's coming our way, and you'll need every hand that can hold a gun if we're to survive the night."

Carter gave the bodyguard one last appraising look from the doorway. "If I ask for your help tonight, god knows we’re truly fucked.” As he closed the door and turned the lock, Ash bellowed in frustration.

CHAPTER TWELVE

Carter leaned out the driver's side window and touched his room pass to the proximity card reader at the exit. The mechanism emitted a short beep, then the car park roller door shuddered into motion, starting to slowly rise. He fidgeted at the bulletproof vest he'd donned prior to getting in the ute; the damn things always seemed to pinch under his left armpit. Although he wasn't expecting to come under fire in the retrieval, the vest would act as a slash-proof garment against Soul Feeder talons.

Icy wind gusted through the gap beneath the roller door, carrying a dusting of snow that melted on contact with the concrete flooring. Carter closed his window and turned up the heater as a shiver worked down his neck.

"Come on," muttered Rylan under her breath.

Carter glanced at his partner from the corner of his eye. She sat bolt upright in the passenger seat, wound tight as a steel spring. Door finally open, Carter put the ute in drive, launching the vehicle into motion. It was still bright outside, but the sun had well and truly begun its descent to the western horizon. Sunset would be at 17:30, giving them less than an hour and a half to find the skier and get back before darkness fell. Down the slope from the lodge, another train full of guests pulled out from the station, starting their descent to safety.

"Hey, I forgot to thank you earlier," said Carter.

Rylan looked at him, one eyebrow slightly raised in question.

"It was an excellent shot." Carter kept his eyes on the road. "A few moments more and it would have had me."

"Maybe, maybe not," said Rylan with a shrug, looking keen to change the topic. She pointed to a road up ahead. "Take the next left. If we stay on that one, it's another six kilometres to the storage hut we need."

Carter slowed to take the corner before accelerating again, pushing the unwieldly vehicle to its limit on the slippery surface. Behind them, their rifles and a box of packed magazines waited for use. Wanting to avoid thinking about the coming fight for a few minutes more, Carter fired off another question, seeing if he could get anything more than a two word answer from his colleague.

"How long have you been with the Cryptid Investigation Unit?"

"Since the beginning," said Rylan, looking out the window. "I finally got support to launch it back in the 1980s."

"Eighties? We were both kids then."

Rylan coughed a humourless laugh. "Ah, I meant early last decade. The concept was first floated back in the '80s. I was just the lucky bastard who got to breathe life into the plan."

"So this is your baby, eh?" said Carter, a note of admiration in his voice. "How the hell did you convince the brass to give you cash for something like this? I mean, I know now that it's legit, but I imagine saying there were dangerous undiscovered creatures roaming the country went down like a sack of shit the first time you pitched it. Am I right?"

Rylan coughed a rough laugh. "Yeah, something like that." She touched a hand to her neck, itching at the skin for a moment. "I gave them irrefutable proof. Once they saw an evolutionary anomaly with their own eyes and the potential risks it posed, they couldn't refuse."

"What creature did you present? Anything like these bastard Soul Feeders?"

"Nah. Something much older."

"Come on, stop dancing around the subject," said Carter. "What was it?"

Rylan turned to look him in the eye. "Look, you last out the mission and maybe I'll tell you the full story." She leaned forward and turned the heater down again before unzipping the neck of her jacket. "Jesus, any hotter in here and I'll bloody melt."

Carter glanced at her, doing a double take as he caught a glimpse of her neck down to the collarbone. Where red, lumpy tissue had existed back in the hotel, there was nothing more than a faint silvery scar.

"That mark on your neck healed quick."

Rylan's eyes narrowed slightly as she stared straight ahead, ignoring his words. Now Carter was properly intrigued. He knew what he'd seen, and wounds didn't heal in the space of hours in the real world. Outside, snow started to billow down in flurries across the steep road, almost obliterating his view for seconds at a time. He switched on the windscreen wipers and leaned forward, rubbing at the fogged glass.

"And what was all that shit from Ash about cutting your throat? He looked like he'd seen a ghost when you walked through the door. In my experience, blokes like him don't scare that easily."

"For fucks sake, Carter, keep your attention on the road."

Through the next flurry of snow, a sharp bend approached rapidly.

Shit.

Carter took his foot off the accelerator, avoiding the temptation to jam on the brake which would guarantee a slide. He eased the ute around the corner, the back wheels skidding sideways before gripping just shy of a cliff at the road's edge.

As the ute straightened out again, Rylan let out a held breath. "Let's get this skier back to the lodge and if there's time, we'll talk."

***

"There's the turn off," said Rylan, pointing ahead to the left.

Carter clocked the wooden sign and slowed. Almost hidden by a low hanging branch, it indicated Hut Three was a hundred metres off the main track. Carter turned the wheel, the ute bucking over the ditch to access the smaller trail. Green branches heavy with snow slapped the windows to either side. He'd have to hope like hell there was a spot to turn the vehicle around, because if he had to reverse out while under attack, it was going to be a nightmare. Tree shadows stretched long, casting the snow in grey as the sun neared the horizon. Time was against them.

"Shit," muttered Carter, bringing the ute to a stop at the tree line.

Undergrowth and trees had been cleared in a thirty metre circumference about the storage hut. But where the ground should have been covered in a pristine blanket of white, something unnatural had taken its place.

The hut was surrounded by a writhing sea of brown. Taloned limbs clicked together as monstrous insects climbed over each other, desperate to reach the front of the pack. The metal sheeting of the hut walls looked like it wouldn't last much longer. Graffitied with sharp scratches, multiple panels were buckled, looking ready to collapse at any moment. A rolling trill of cicada-like noise emanated from the throng of insects, fluctuating in volume like a Mexican wave around a stadium, growing to eardrum bursting intensity before easing once again.

"Fuck, they're in the trees as well," said Rylan.

Carter glanced up, and caught sight of a Soul Feeder bursting through the back of a nymph's shell to emerge glistening wet and ready to feast. They needed to get moving before the hut was completely covered in the bastards.

A few creatures at the back of the pack had noticed their arrival, breaking away to investigate. He opened his door, grabbed the rifle from behind his seat and took aim, squeezing off single shots to drop the closest insects. On the other side of the ute, Rylan joined in, face grim as she targeted those at the back of the pack.

A huge clang sounded from behind, the vehicle shuddering as a Soul Feeder thudded onto the ute's tray from one of the nearby trees. Carter spun on his heel to take on the new threat, squeezing his trigger as the beast lunged over the cabin's roof. The creature screamed as its taloned hand disintegrated in a bloody mist. Carter changed aim, his second round catching the beast through its open mouth, smashing it backward to sprawl in the snow. He turned back around, and saw that they'd succeeded in drawing attention away from the hut.

Maybe too well.

Venom drooled from pincers, dripping onto the snow as a dozen Soul Feeders stalked toward their ute. Carter caught sight of movement in his peripheral vision, a streak of brown as yet more of the beasts sought to get behind their position.

"We're getting flanked!" yelled Carter, swivelling to track one of the creatures and squeeze off a shot. Leaving Rylan to cover the other direction, he concentrated his fire toward their rear. Allowing his body to go on auto, he calmly fired upon one beast after another, barely two seconds between each round. Orange blood splattered the ground around each Soul Feeder corpse he sent to the grave.

"The door's clear, time to move," shouted Rylan before ducking back into the passenger door and slamming it shut.

Carter followed suit. Passing his rifle across to Rylan, he slid behind the driver's wheel and stamped on the accelerator. Snow spurted from behind the ute before the tyre chains gripped. Lurching forward, the ute caught two beasts on the bull bar, driving them under the wheels with a dull crunch of fractured exoskeletons.

He spun the wheel, driving the ute in an arc to come at the hut from side on. Soul Feeders came at them from all directions, attacking with suicidal abandon, hitting with force enough to rock the cabin. A thump sounded from above, the roof buckling downwards beneath the weight of another creature.

Carter skidded to a halt next to the door, smashing the last two persistent Soul Feeders away from the building. Their bodies hit the snow ten paces distant, legs snapped and torsos crushed from the impact. With the trauma sustained, the creatures should have stayed down, and yet they rolled over and dragged themselves back toward the ute with their arms, leaking internal fluids as they came. The snow before the hut was a slurry of blood, excrement and mud. The back door of the twin cab was mere inches away from the hut's door. Carter hit the horn, a long blast that he hoped the skier would understand.

"Come on!" he muttered through clenched teeth.

Finally, the door opened a crack, a terrified man peeking through before throwing it wide. Rylan reached behind and wound down the back window for the skier to climb through. The man dove into the gap, legs hanging ungainly for a moment as Rylan helped to drag him in.

The creature on the roof changed position, metal buckling with every step. Carter aimed his handgun upwards, and unloaded three quick shots. In response, a talon stabbed through the thin metal. Black, glistening and long as a sword, the tip opened the skin down the back of his shoulder like a razor blade, grating across the bone.

Carter grunted with pain, jammed the barrel of his pistol against the roof and shot again. The Soul Feeder screamed and tumbled forward, smashing onto the windscreen before landing on the bonnet, a web of cracks spreading across the glass.

"He's in. GO, GO, GO!" shouted Rylan.

Carter stomped on the accelerator, the car bucking over a series of carcasses as it lurched away from the hut. The beast he'd shot through the roof refused to be dislodged. Gripping the hood with bony fingers, the Soul Feeder drew itself up to the windscreen and screamed at them, rancid saliva flecked with blood spraying the glass. It lunged forward with pincers splayed, the venomous spikes punching two small holes through the windscreen. Poison squirted through the gaps, melting the plastic of the dash where they fell. The Soul Feeder raised a fist and punched the glass, fine cracks arcing out from the impact point. With his view obstructed, Carter could only pray he wasn't driving straight for a tree.

"Shoot the prick for God's sake!" he shouted.

Rylan brought her rifle to bear with difficulty in the cramped space, muzzle touching the windscreen as she fired a spurt of rounds. Glass exploded like shrapnel, hitting Carter's face in a hail of stinging fragments. He hit the brakes, bringing the ute to a skidding halt. The

Soul Feeder slid off the hood in a bloody mess as Rylan kicked out the remaining glass. Further trills and eerie chirps sounded from behind. Carter glanced over his shoulder to see more of the beasts emerge from the far tree line.

How many of the damn things are there?

The man they'd rescued was bloodied and trembling. He hunched forward on the back seat, clutching the shredded remains of his right hand. Thumb, index and middle finger were missing, bitten off in a crescent-shaped wound.

Ears stunned and whining from the gunfire, Carter put the ute in gear and accelerated for home. Freezing wind howled through the smashed windscreen, needling exposed skin like a sadist. As he hit the main trail, the sun finally dipped below the horizon, plunging the mountain into twilight. Carter drove as fast as he dared on the slick road. The chasing Soul Feeders gradually slipped back, finally merging with shadows.

They were free for now, but it did little to improve Carter's mood. He shrugged his injured shoulder gingerly, the laceration burning at the movement, warm blood leaking afresh down his back. They were running low on ammunition, with no idea of how many Soul Feeders were in pursuit. And when the next battle was joined, the beasts would have the advantage of night.

Carter stubbornly pushed the thought to the back of his mind and concentrated on keeping wheels upon the road.

CHAPTER THIRTEEN

Ash flexed against the zip-ties, every muscle straining as he sought to escape the restraints. The chair creaked from the tension. He pushed harder, teeth grinding and face red with effort. A trickle of blood dripped from his left hand as the band of plastic cut into his wrist, slicing through the skin with a razor's kiss. He hissed at the pain, sagging back as he gave up.

The ties weren't going to break.

All he'd achieve was slicing through tendons if he kept up the attempt, and he needed his fingers working to hold a knife against that damn agent's neck.

Fucking bitch.

Risen from the dead like a bloody demon, she'd surprised him all right. Who wouldn't have been caught off guard? All that crap she'd spouted about a bulletproof vest was bullshit. He'd buried his knife deep under her ribs, seen agony on her face as he twisted the blade. Not to mention cutting her throat. Hell, he still wore the blood that had spurted from her carotid arteries. In a career that spanned British military black ops, to mercenary warfare in the heart of Africa, Ash had seen some weird shit over the years. But a corpse rising from the dead? That topped the rest by a clear mile.

Ash's head jerked up at the sound of a key in the door. The handle turned and suddenly his boss, Freidman, burst into the room. The man looked ready to murder someone, face red, fat jowls beneath his chin like a bullfrog as he pinned him with a furious gaze.

"I have a pair of government agents stomping around *my* hotel, ordering *my* staff about as if they own the damned place. And where do I find you, but sitting on your arse!" Freidman's gaze dropped, taking in the ties about his ankles and wrists. "You've got to be kidding me…" he muttered, shaking his head. "When I paid for your services, I was assured you were the best."

Ash clenched his jaw for a moment, forcing himself not to bite. "There was extenuating circumstances. If you could clip these ties, sir, I have news to report."

Freidman's lips thinned, looking as if he'd tasted something foul. For a second, Ash thought the old creep was about to turn and leave him strapped to the chair, but he eventually picked up a pair of trauma scissors. Designed for cutting through clothes, the blades severed the tough plastic bands like paper.

At the release of pressure, blood flooded back into his fingers and feet with an intense sting of pins and needles. Ash clenched his teeth at the pain, flexing his fingers open and closed until the sensation began to ease. Blood welled afresh from the laceration at his wrist as he examined the wound. He spread the margins wide and was relieved to see nothing but yellow globular fat cells at the bottom. The cable tie hadn't bitten deep enough to damage any of his tendons. After a brief search through cabinets mounted on the left side of the room, he found a pad of gauze and bandage to wrap the wound and stop it bleeding.

"Did you find what we wanted up on the mountain?" asked Freidman.

A sideways glance at the billionaire confirmed a change in mood. The mottled veneer of rage had seeped out of the man's face, replaced by cold intensity. As long as Ash brought the bastard a chance of increased wealth, everything would be forgiven.

Ash nodded and unzipped the tarpaulin bag, exposing the mash of gore-drenched body parts within. One side of the opening flopped down, allowing a stream of orange blood and clot to escape and spatter the floor. "The beast was right where they'd said it would be. It was too tall to fit in the bag intact, so I had to do a little dicing to bring him back."

Freidman leaned over the bag, lip curled in disgust as his gaze roamed over the mess within. "And what's on top? It seems to be a separate intact creature."

"Aye, boss, you're right," sighed Ash. "And there lies our problem," he said, pointing at the dog-sized insect. "It crawled out of the ground before climbing a tree to shed its skin. The evidence points towards it being a nymph stage of the big bastard."

Freidman curled his hands into fists as the news sunk in. "So, they're not long-lived like we'd hoped."

"No. Merely a freakish insect with an abnormally long nymph stage underground. No idea how long they live above the surface, but most things like this emerge to feed, fuck, lay eggs and die off. Chances are, they won't be any different. And there's lots more where this came from. Hundreds of the beasts are digging their way to the surface as we speak."

The billionaire turned away and walked slowly to the metal doors of the body fridge at the end of the room. Without warning he suddenly kicked out, buckling a steel panel. Again and again he kicked in wordless fury. Ash waited calmly, allowing his employer to burn off anger, content that it was directed somewhere other than himself. Eventually, Freidman stumbled back to a chair and slumped. He breathed quickly, but despite his body's exhaustion at the spurt of activity, his eyes still burned with rage.

"There will be no scientific breakthrough. My guests have been slaughtered and the grand launch of my alpine resort is a failure. The press will have a god damned field day," he spat.

"All may not be a waste, sir," said Ash quietly. The billionaire's eyes jerked up, the businessman's instinct catching his tone of voice, like a tiger latching onto the scent of prey.

"Out with it," he snapped.

Ash smiled on the inside, knowing he had the man's attention. "I've found a better candidate to examine than these disgusting beasts. A *human* candidate who can heal at phenomenal rates and spit in the Grim Reaper's face."

Freidman eyed him calmly. "If you're fucking with me, I'll have your balls cut off and shoved down your throat."

Ash had enough experience working for the man to know it wasn't an idle threat. He pulled a chair next to Freidman and began to systematically detail his encounter with Agent Rylan. Eventually he rocked back in this chair, story complete.

"You're positively sure?" asked Freidman. "The most likely explanation is that you had a psychotic episode and imagined the whole fantasy."

"I know what I saw," growled Ash. "When I cut Rylan's throat, I sliced through carotid and jugular vessels on both sides of her neck. No-one, and I mean *no-one*, lives through a mortal wound like that to fight another day."

"And yet your agent did," mused Freidman, his eyes now distant as he considered Ash's story.

"So, what do you want to do, boss?"

Freidman focused again upon Ash, the rage of minutes earlier a distant memory. "We take Agent Rylan alive and move her off-shore. I have a hidden research facility in Columbia where study can begin upon the specimen."

"And her soldier buddy?"

"Kill him if need be, I'll leave it to your judgment. I've requested the attendance of my private chopper, it should be on site in four hours. Plenty of time for you to nab our prize, wouldn't you say?"

***

Rylan shouldered open the door to the hotel lobby and dumped a half-empty crate of magazines on the tiled floor. Ice-laden wind billowed through the gap as she held the door for Carter and the Norwegian skier to enter. Supported by Carter's arm about his waist, the skier was more injured than she'd first thought. Aside from the trauma to his hand, one of the creatures had skewered his lower abdomen, punching a hole front to back. In the short drive down the mountain his colour had deteriorated markedly. Pale skin, increased breath rate and thready pulse were tell-tale signs of traumatic blood loss that needed an operating theatre. If he didn't make it to a hospital soon, Arvid's next stop would be the morgue.

"Good to see you made it back, I was starting to get a little concerned," said Ash, a mocking grin on his face as he swaggered around the corner from the main atrium, trailed by Freidman.

Rylan looked up, eyes narrowing at the sight of the billionaire and his attack hound.

"Could have sworn I left you under arrest?"

Freidman raised his hands in a parody of contrition. "Now, now, Agent. If someone must be blamed for that, it is me. But your partner gave the order to evacuate, and I couldn't possibly condone leaving a trusted employee to be slaughtered by the hellish beasts of this mountain."

"How *noble* of you, sir," said Rylan, pulling a second pair of zip-cuffs from an inside pocket. "But I prefer my dogs on a leash, especially ones that have already bared their teeth."

"Back off with those cuffs, Agent." Ash's smile stayed fixed below dead eyes. "How about we all stay friends for the evening, be a shame to see you get hurt again."

"Boss, as much as I hate to say it, we've got bigger fish to fry," said Carter. "When that horde catches up, we're going to need every hand that can hold a gun."

"Even better if that set of hands knows how to aim and shoot," said Ash. "Listen to your colleague, Agent Rylan. The man's talking sense."

Rylan took a slow breath, then slipped the zip-cuffs back in her jacket and stepped close to Carter. "If he betrays us, it's on your head."

Carter gave her a stiff nod, then eased the skier to a seat. He walked behind the reception, ripped a fire-evacuation map off the wall and brought it to the front of the desk.

"When did the last train of guests head down the mountain?" asked Rylan.

"Thirty minutes ago," said Freidman.

"Good. Radio through and tell them to keep it at the base station. Using the train isn't an option for us, we'd risk attracting the creatures in our wake to more victims. We have to make a stand here, work out a way to wipe them out."

Ash leaned over the map, pointing at the main bar. "That's your place to do it. The bar faces up the mountain, so will probably be the first point of contact. There's a balcony off the front that stands a couple of metres off the ground, might help to keep the bastards at arm's length for a bit longer."

"How many rounds have we got?" asked Carter.

"Not a whole lot, we didn't come armed for a war," said Rylan. "There's half a dozen mags left for the rifles. Same again for the handguns. If we run out before the show's over, we're going to need a fall-back position."

Carter traced a finger on the map from the bar to the large room behind it. "That's the main auditorium, right? The map shows it as a single fire compartment. That means heavy fire doors can be locked at all exit points from the room?"

Freidman nodded. "What are you getting at, Agent?"

Carter hooked a finger for them to follow and jogged from the reception area to the area in question. "If we can attract the last of the horde into this room, it should hold them long enough to finish the job."

Fire doors, and a locked room. A smile kinked Rylan's mouth as she caught onto her partner's line of thought. "You want to burn them?"

Carter nodded. "We take fuel stored for the emergency generator and soak the floors, ready to go. All it would take is one of us to strike a match and leave the beasts to fry."

"No. I forbid it," snapped Freidman. "I've spent over five-hundred million dollars building this resort, and you want to burn it to the ground? Are you mad?"

"Use your head," said Rylan. "The blaze should be contained within the fire compartment, stopping spread to other sectors of the hotel and limiting the damage. Once the insects are burnt, we turn on the sprinkler system to extinguish the flames."

"It's insured, right?" said Carter.

"They've got a point, boss," said Ash reluctantly.

Freidman threw his hands in the air, spouting a stream of obscenities as he walked back toward reception, leaving the group behind.

"I guess he won't be helping?" said Carter.

Rylan smirked at the thought of how much cash the evil prick was about to lose. "We haven't got long, let's get moving."

CHAPTER FOURTEEN

The skier looked like shit. Fringe stuck to his forehead in ringlets of cold sweat, skin grey. Arvid had initially watched them work with pained intensity, but his eyes had become unfocused, staring into space as he grunted shallow breaths on the floor. Carter had seen too many comrades in the same state while waiting for retrieval from the field—few had survived.

"He hasn't got long."

Rylan shot him a withering glance from where she knelt at the victim's side. "Hot tip, if you've got nothing useful to relay, shut the fuck up." She pulled a vial of morphine from the disaster medical kit Freidman had unlocked for them, snapped the lid off and began drawing the liquid into a syringe. "Stating the damn obvious is a waste of time."

Carter grit his teeth. "I might be new to this unit, but I've done my time. Don't talk to me like I'm a kid."

Rylan barked a humourless laugh. "When you get to my age, you're all like children." She buried the syringe into the skier's thigh and injected the morphine. "Finish sorting the bar. Once Arvid's out of pain, I'll be right behind you."

Carter forced a slow breath. Letting the woman get on his nerves was stupid. If they made it through the night, he'd raise patterns of communication in the debrief. Until then, he had more important things at hand.

An acrid stink of kerosene filled his nose, making him cough. A thud of plastic hitting tiles echoed from the atrium, and Carter turned to see an empty jerry can skid across the floor in the distance, thrown aside by Ash. Elegant armchairs and couches that had once dotted the vast room were now clustered in the middle, a mountain of fuel for the coming bonfire. The bodyguard unscrewed another jerry can's lid and upended it, pouring its contents carefully over the upholstery, then in widening circles about the chairs.

Carter jogged back to the bar area, quickly dragging the last of the tables and chairs into stacked groups. If they were forced back from their initial perch on the balcony, Carter wanted to herd the beasts into a bottle neck of concentrated fire within the bar area. Anything that slowed them down and contributed to a higher casualty to rounds ratio played into their favour. He carried a holstered pistol, while his rifle hung over his shoulder on its sling. The other rifles and ammunition were stored at the balcony ready for use.

"You know your colleague's a monster, right?"

Carter glanced over his shoulder, frown deepening as he found Ash standing close behind. The prick had the stealth of a feral cat, he hadn't heard a noise of the bodyguard's approach.

"I haven't got time for this shit. If you're finished with the atrium, can you take a station on the balcony and keep watch?"

He might as well have said nothing for all the notice Ash took.

"You're a government organisation hunting cryptids, and yet you don't even realise you've got one as a partner." He pointed out the window to the darkness of the mountain. "The beasts that are about to attack us? They're pretty grim, I'll give you that. But at least they stay dead when you kill them. Agent Rylan doesn't even obey that basic law of nature. If I was you, I'd keep my distance from the freak."

Carter clenched a fist, knuckles whitening. The shit was about to hit the fan, and all everyone wanted to do was create more drama. The distraction was going to see them killed. "What the fuck are you talking about?"

"I killed Rylan this morning. Sunk a blade under her ribs to the hilt before slitting her throat. Nothing personal mind you, just business," he said without a shred of discernible conscience. "Freidman did a background check on you, mate. You're ex-special forces, and have probably done your fair share of wet work. When you're that close to your enemy, there's no mistaking a mortal wound, especially when they die in your arms."

Carter grimaced. "I'm nothing like you. When I killed, it was by the rules of war; I never took a person's life for money."

Ash laughed, and for the first time the smile actually reached his eyes. "You keep telling yourself that, sunshine. Pretty sure all us soldiers got a pay check, ain't no-one putting their lives on the line for charity. We're all paid killers, the rest is just semantics and personal justification." Ash snorted back and spat a yellow glob of phlegm onto the carpet. "But that's beside the point. I killed your boss, and she rose from the dead with her injuries healed. Come the end of this fight, she will need to be stopped. The possible consequences of her falling into the wrong hands are hideous. I mean, can you imagine fighting an army of her type?"

Carter's heart grew cold at the thought. He'd seen Rylan's neck change from an ugly new wound to the faded white of an old scar in the space of twenty minutes. His gut told him something was deeply odd about his partner, but he'd boxed his concerns for a later date. If Ash was right, Rylan's secret to healing and ongoing life could change the art of war, tip the balance of power on its head and negate the politician's numbers game. There'd be no more worrying about the next election if a war claimed too many lives. In his mind he saw slain soldiers rising from the bloody dust, virtually unstoppable.

"If I stood aside," said Carter, "what would you do with her?"

A metallic click of a round being chambered sounded from the entrance to the bar.

***

The skier gave her a slight nod, his lips mouthing 'thank you' before closing his eyes. Arvid's breathing slowed, his chest barely moving. A few minutes more and he'd be wherever normal humans went at death. Rylan didn't believe in a god, had never seen a white light or felt a comforting presence when she'd passed beyond the veil. In fact, she never recalled anything between the agony of death, to the sudden awakening. The exquisite pain of partially healed wounds on opening her eyes was usually enough to distract any thoughts of the afterlife. If there was something after death, she supposed it was a void of indifference; a reservoir of energy without concept of good or bad, ready for insertion to a new vessel to restart the cycle.

Freidman sat behind the reception of his hotel, refusing to help. Whenever she glanced his way, he was always watching. Staring. Eyes fixed on her head with what she could have sworn was avarice. She put the old creep out of mind and checked her watch.

Fifteen minutes had passed since Ash had gone running for the fuel and they'd started to enact their plan.

The first beasts could be on them any minute and they needed to be ready with rifles in hand. She would survive anything thrown her way, but if the swarm chopped them to pieces and continued down the valley, hundreds of innocent people would not be so lucky.

Rylan drew her weapon as she walked toward the front bar, and as she got closer, heard muted anger as Ash and her partner talked quickly. When Carter finally responded after a brief silence, her heart sank with disappointment.

And he'd seemed decent.

She chambered a round and stepped around the doorway, muzzle aimed at the bodyguard's centre of mass.

"This looks a little cosy, boys," said Rylan, her voice low. "I hope Ash isn't putting foolish ideas in your head, *partner*."

Ash jumped at her voice, his face blanching a little as he stared at her gun. "No need to get testy, love. We were just discussing the coming attack."

Carter glanced sideways at the bodyguard, lip curled in disgust. "This issue with the rapid healing of your neck, we need to clear it up, fast. The merc seems to think you're a Lazarus. And with all the shit I've seen today, I'm hard pressed to turn a blind eye."

"What, so you're going to side with this low life?"

Carter's lips narrowed. "I never said that. But, I *do* want the truth. If we're to work as partners, there can't be mission compromising secrets like this."

Rylan looked between the two of them for a moment. It would be so easy to walk away, leave them to the shitstorm barrelling down the mountain in a maelstrom of claws and pincers. She started to turn away, then stopped herself and holstered her pistol. Rylan shrugged off her jacket and rolled one sleeve to her elbow in quick, precise movements. In the blink of an eye, a combat knife appeared in the opposite hand, a sleight of hand so quick it would have stunned a close-up magician.

"Carter, you wanted to know how I convinced the head of ASIO to launch a Cryptid Investigation Unit? It took no more than this."

Rylan drew the blade down the back of her forearm twice, creating an elliptical shape like a narrow, elongated eye. Blood welled from the wound as she sheathed the knife, then dug her fingers into the skin at the edge of the wound. Gritting her teeth against the searing pain, she ripped the skin and a layer of fat away with a sound of tearing cotton. She flicked the bloody mess into the corner, crimson trickling from the corner of her mouth where she'd bitten the side of her cheek to stop herself screaming.

Both men stared at her in horror, eyes wide, mouths slightly open.

"Jesus, it's starting to heal," said Carter quietly.

Rylan glanced down, knowing the process had already started. The pain had lessened somewhat as blood vessels sealed and nerve endings began to regenerate. Across the exposed fascia of her forearm muscles, a layer of fat grew at speed, spreading like a wave from the outsides of the wound to centre. Raw, new skin followed it, bright pink like a sunburn. In the space of fifty seconds, the wound was sealed again.

"Deeper wounds involving multiple structures take longer."

Carter ran a hand through his hair, cheeks puffed out as he exhaled. "So it's true. When you get killed, how long until you take another breath?"

Rylan shrugged. "I think it varies on the trauma. Sometimes it's minutes, others take longer."

"All this dying and coming back—is this why you're such a short tempered, cranky SOB?" asked Carter with a half-smile.

"Try fighting your way through a man's world for *three hundred years*. I think I've earnt the right to get annoyed by people's bullshit every now and then."

Rylan turned to Ash. "You got lucky last time, mate. I didn't think you were unhinged enough to stab a federal agent out of the blue." She drew her gun, a set of zip-ties appearing in the other hand. "But it won't happen again. I won't have you pointing a gun at my back while we fight, so let's get your wrists back in a set of these, eh?"

Ash looked ready to bolt, his eyes flicking between her, Carter and the exit to the atrium. "Don't fucking do it, Ash. I'll just put a bullet in your leg if you run. Make it a whole lot easier for those bugs to catch you."

A shout echoed from the reception area. "They're here!"

Fuck.

There was no time to mess with the bloody merc now. Rylan darted past him, burying a sharp elbow in his side to shove him out of the way. She rounded the bar's door to see the skier dragging himself backwards. Freidman scurried from behind the reception, nearly tripping over Arvid as he ran for the lift at the end of the atrium.

Rylan lifted her gun, aiming past him to the front doors. "Where are they?!"

Sweat soaked dark patches beneath the billionaire's armpits, his pupils dilated and eyes wide. He pointed over his shoulder while barely slowing his stride. "Outside, you fool. I have a helicopter inbound. I'll wait for ten minutes after the fire is lit, but after that, you're on your own."

A shadow loomed at the front entrance, tall and thin. A sabre-like claw extended toward the glass, tapped upon it, then drew down the surface with a high pitched squeal.

Rylan's head flicked around at the sound of shattering glass in the bar.

"CONTACT!" shouted Carter.

Automatic gunfire turned the night to chaos.

CHAPTER FITEEN

Carter's heart lurched at movement in his peripheral vision. A streak of black careered over the tables on the balcony outside, making straight for the main window. Glass exploded in a spray of diamonds as the first Soul Feeder careened through. The beast crashed into a wooden long table, flipping the massive weight of timber as if no more than plastic. Bright lights of the bar lit the huge insect's exoskeleton, swirls of brown, black and ochre red standing proud under the glare. Multifaceted eyes scanned the room before locking upon the two men. Pincers to either side of its fanged mouth spread wide, venom erupting in a premature spurt of excitement down its chest.

"CONTACT!"

Carter's body went on autopilot, years of training and muscle memory operating his body by instinct alone. He thumped the butt of his rifle into his shoulder and fired a three shot burst, catching the beast in the centre of its chest. The rounds hit with the force of a sledgehammer, knocking the creature back two steps as a ragged hole appeared in its armoured thorax. Carter's next round went higher, plunging through an open mouth to spray its brainstem across the floor behind. The beast crashed back, hitting the ground in a twitching mass of limbs before falling still.

Carter darted around the fallen monster, making for the outside balcony. His shoes crunched on broken glass as he stepped through the shattered window. The outside seated area of the bar held numerous long tables lined by bench seats. In less violent times, the seats would be filled by guests in winter jackets, sipping hot chocolates, or drinking from tall steins of beer as they took in the magnificent alpine views. But this evening was a different matter. He and Rylan had shoved the tables to the side earlier, clearing a fighting area before the safety rail.

A dusting of snow covered the timber decking, his feet leaving dark prints in the white as he strode to the forward railing. Freezing wind numbed his face as he squinted into the dark, rifle at his shoulder, scanning for the next threat. In the past hour the temperature had plunged well below zero, the night air sucking body heat like a parasite. The clouds of earlier had fled, leaving a sky of stars and a spotlight moon in their wake. Ski runs, cast in cold monotones of grey, wound down the mountain like vasculature between the dark forest. As Carter's eyes adjusted, his skin prickled with goosebumps that had nothing to do with the cold. The forest was on the move, bulging forward, spilling in a sea of jointed legs onto the cleared ground before the resort.

There were too many.

Even if he scored a kill with every round, there would be no way to turn the tide. He glanced to the south where the train line finished at the bottom of the valley. The buildings holding the evacuated guests were a bright sparkle in the pitch dark, a light that would draw the beasts onward if they weren't stopped. He grit his teeth and stared ahead again. It might seem impossible, but he had to believe otherwise. Victories had been won against seemingly insurmountable odds. Defeat was only guaranteed if no one held the line, and Carter would ensure that didn't happen.

"Give me a rifle."

He looked over his shoulder, saw Ash standing at the verge of a broken window.

"What, for you to shoot me in the back?" Even if Carter understood the merc's concerns with Rylan, it didn't mean he trusted him.

"The enemy of my enemy is my friend. You know it's true."

But only until the common threat is gone. Carter was no fool. "Fine, grab a rifle," he growled.

Ash took up a stance four metres to his right, elbow propped on the safety rail to steady his aim.

They weren't far off now, already within firing distance, but not yet close enough for guaranteed hits. "Save your ammo until they pass the base of the chairlift, we need a kill with every bullet."

"And I thought the SAS could shoot?" taunted Ash as he chambered his first round. "That can't be more than a hundred yards."

Carter ignored him as he stared over his sights. The topic was moot anyway as the forward line of beasts surged underneath the chairlift. The muted thunder of their limbs pounding the snow sounded like a stampede as Carter picked his first target and squeezed the trigger. A split second later, the Soul Feeder dropped with half its head missing, tripping two others in a tangle of limbs. The gunfire stoked the beast's anger, and as one they released a high-pitched scream of rage that made Carter's eardrums crackle painfully.

Beside him, Ash took down his own first victim, and then another. Both men kept their rifles set to single shot. One considered round every two seconds with metronomic regularity. For those shots that failed to kill a beast outright, there was no time to finish the job, not when others surged forward at ten times the speed of their injured cousins. The Soul Feeders closed the distance rapidly through the hail of lead. Carter swore under his breath as he missed a shot, wasting a second round on the same beast. Some zigzagged, others advanced straight as an arrow, making it difficult to track individuals through the mess.

"Where the hell is Rylan?" shouted Ash.

To Carter's stunned eardrums, the merc's shout barely registered. He spared the barest second to flick a searching look backward into the building for his partner, his gut dropping as he saw the carapace of a Soul Feeder streak past the door to the atrium.

Fuck.

If the insects had found a different way into the hotel, it was only a matter of time before they were flanked. Carter swallowed, his mouth dry as a camel's hoof as he turned back to the advancing swarm, picked his next target and squeezed the trigger.

***

Rylan dropped to a crouch behind the arm of a couch. "Arvid, don't move a muscle."

The skier stopped dragging himself and lay flat, eyes clamped shut and biting his lip hard enough that a drop of blood rolled down his chin. Rylan peered over the top of the couch, hand on the butt of her gun, hoping like hell the creature would move on if it didn't see anything worth attacking. She had no idea how its eyes and brain worked, whether they relied upon movement to trigger an attack response. The last thing she needed was to fight a battle on two fronts, and with luck it would be drawn by the gunfire to join its brethren.

The creature leaned forward, bringing its eyes close to the glass door. It flinched from the bright light before growing accustomed and searching the interior. Rylan ducked as its empty gaze swept toward her, then on to the Norwegian. Unlike her, he was lying in plain sight at the bottom of a wall, just past the bar's entrance. Arvid's chest moved quickly in shallow, grunting breaths. One balled fist pushed against his leaking abdomen as a groan of agony escaped his lips.

The beast froze, gaze flicking toward the skier again as it cocked its head to the side.

Come on, keep it together.

Arvid vomited. His body convulsed as a tide of crimson erupted from his mouth, emptying a stomach full of gore in a bloody gout before falling limp, his pain finally at an end. Huge pincers to either side of the beast's jaw spread wide as it bared fangs and launched at the door. Exoskeleton crunched into the metal frame, tearing two hinges from the door jamb as the glass shattered within the bottom panel. The beast crouched down, diving through the smaller gap and into the reception area.

Rylan drew her gun, chambered a round and fired over the top of the couch. The bullet missed, only creasing a line in the chitin armour at the side of its torso. It was enough to draw the creature's attention away from the skier. On all fours, it stared at her and emitted a harsh tinny chirp, the sound bouncing off the walls of the room painfully. It flexed its legs down, like a spring coiled ready for release.

Knowing she was seen, there was no point hiding any longer. Rylan stood, feet in a wide stance as she raised her weapon and squeezed the trigger. Instead of jumping straight at her, the beast dived to the side, her bullet chipping plaster where it had been a split second earlier. The creature's bony feet crunched against the wall, hitting it with body horizontal to the ground before launching once again, leaving deep gouges in the plaster.

This time it leapt straight for her. It came in a blur, a missile of psychopathic claws and teeth. Rylan fell backward, tracking it with her gun to fire three times rapidly.

This time her aim was true, each round punching ragged holes through exoskeleton of torso and head. Dead before it hit the ground, it clattered to the floor and smacked into Arvid's side. Rylan rolled to her feet and ran forward, touching a finger below the angle of the Norwegian's jaw to feel for a pulse.

Nothing. He was gone.

A steady roll of gunfire echoed from the bar's balcony. She was needed elsewhere. Leaving the skier to stare sightlessly at the roof, Rylan darted into the bar. Taking in the wreckage of the window and dead beast with a glance, she scooped up the last rifle on the run, jammed home a magazine and stepped through broken glass to the balcony.

After the bright light of the reception area, outside seemed near pitch black. Seeing a set of light switches on the outside wall, Rylan ran her hand down them, flicking each one on. Light flooded from several spotlights above, illuminating the surrounding snow and bush in a harsh glare.

At the sudden brightness, Carter looked over his shoulder at her and gave a tight nod of recognition. "I don't think we're going to hold them for long. Where's Freidman?"

"He's gone for the roof to wait for his helicopter."

Carter fired a three round burst. "Okay. Take the left wing, the bastards are coming in thick!"

Rylan skidded to a halt before the safety rail with rifle already at her shoulder, feet sliding on the snow-covered floorboards. The ground below was a heaving mass of jointed limbs, carapace and fangs. Huge insects crawled over their dead siblings and would soon be within leaping distance of the balcony. Although no more emerged from the tree line, there had to be at least two hundred of the bastards clawing their way towards dinner. A few at the back of the crowd unfurled little wings to fly, but their ungainly slow movement in the air allowed her to knock them from the sky with ease. After that, the rest stuck to the ground, instead leaping forward with powerful limbs.

Rylan fired at the front line of the advancing mass, her rifle gradually taking a steeper angle until she was almost shooting straight down. Light from the spotlights reflected off the Soul Feeder's eyes, making them glow in the darkness. Rylan took advantage, using the space between each shining set of orbs as a target, decimating one beast after another. Standing at least eight foot tall, a large Soul Feeder flexed downward then leapt, soaring straight up at her. Its arm swung overhead, the sabre-like claw of one hand sinking into the wooden railing for purchase as it pulled itself onto the balcony. Rylan took two involuntary steps backwards, firing almost point-blank into the creature. Orange blood spurted in an arc as the arm separated from the torso at the shoulder. It screamed as it fell, leaving the arm hanging with its talons buried in the woodwork. Another heaved itself above the railing at the same point. Rylan turned her weapon around and lunged forward, smashing the rifle butt into the fragile tissue of its eye. The creature screamed and fell, bony fingers clutched over the ruined orb.

Further along the balcony, Carter ducked, a razor-sharp talon slashing at his face as a beast cleared space at the railing. He stumbled back, ejecting his magazine and reaching for another before coming up empty.

"I'm out," he shouted and let the rifle drop to its strap, drawing his handgun instead to fire on the beast.

"Conserve ammo and fall back!" ordered Rylan.

Instead of arguing for a change, Ash flicked to full auto, firing a swathe of lead across the length of the balcony to give them breathing space, then joined the agents in retreat.

Rylan knelt by the crate of ammunition, clenching her teeth in irritation as she picked out the last two magazines. Throwing the first to Carter to replace his empty, she passed the second reluctantly to the merc as she still had nearly a full magazine remaining.

Rylan hooked her thumb backwards for them to follow and jogged to the rear of the bar, passing quickly through the bottleneck they'd created between mounds of furniture.

"We hold them here, pile some bodies to make it harder for them to follow through the gap, then retreat to the atrium. I don't want you to use more than half the magazine; we'll still need a few rounds up our sleeve, okay?"

Ash grunted acknowledgement before shooting the first beast to crawl over the shattered window frame.

"Wait until they're at the bottleneck," growled Carter, "or you'll give away our advantage."

Ash glared at him and made for the atrium. "You do it then, I'll ready the bonfire. When I see you two exit the bar, I'll be ready to throw the match."

Glad to have the creep away from her, Rylan nodded and turned her attention back to the bottleneck. She took a side-on stance, rifle at her shoulder. Sweat stung as it trickled through an eye and she cuffed it aside with the back of her wrist.

"Incoming!" yelled Carter.

Ears whining from the deafening gunfire of earlier, she grit her teeth and drew a bead on the first creature to enter her line of sight. Seeing her, it dropped to all fours and surged forward, leaping ten feet at a time like a sprinting cheetah. Breath tight in her chest, she forced herself to wait until it was closer before finally pulling the trigger. Her round obliterated half the creature's skull and it dropped like a marionette, sliding to a stop at her feet. Barely even registering the vile creature beneath her, she tracked the next target and fired again.

Within moments, the bodies began to pile up, each shooter forced back step after step to avoid the swiping claws of half-dead monstrosities amongst the heap of corpses blocking the path between heaped tables and chairs. Rylan squeezed her trigger and it clicked on an empty chamber. She swore viciously, realising she'd failed to follow her own instructions.

She was empty.

Rylan shrugged the rifle strap over her head and tossed the now useless weapon aside. "Carter, we need to retreat!"

Waiting until she saw her partner respond and follow, she turned and ran for the atrium.

"Ash! Get ready, it's time to go!"

Rylan skidded to a halt beside the bodyguard at the mound of kerosene soaked furniture. Ash stared at her with rifle in hand, an odd look on his face.

"Where's your rifle? You out of rounds or something?"

She nodded. "Yeah, we need to—"

"Good. Makes my life a little easier."

Rylan recoiled as he lifted the rifle to his shoulder and pulled the trigger. As the echo of the gunshot cleared from her ears, she touched a hand to her chest expecting to find a craterous wound, but there was no damage. Then she realised the merc hadn't been aiming at her.

She pivoted, spinning back around to the bar in time to see Carter slump against the doorway, his hand pressed to his chest, eyes wide with agony and betrayal.

"You fucking bastard!"

"Don't worry, love, the next one's got your name on it."

Rylan's hand dropped to her handgun at her waist, but she was too slow. White hot agony bloomed in her back, and she was punched to the ground by the force of the bullet strike, landing hard on her face.

Fuck, not ag...

CHAPTER SIXTEEN

Carter thumped against the wall outside the bar, stars bursting before his eyes as his head cracked on plaster. Badly winded, his mouth gaped as he tried to draw breath in vain. The two rounds had hit his chest with a stallion's kick, and despite the bulletproof vest under his jacket, he knew he'd busted ribs and probably his sternum. He slid down the wall, fighting to retain consciousness as grey tinged the corners of his vision. Finally he managed to draw breath, the broken ends of his ribs grating together like razor blades. A second shot sounded, and he raised tired eyes just in time to see Rylan pitch onto her face.

He wanted to swear, to rant. To fucking cut a hole in the bastard's heart. But by the time he'd reached his knees, Ash already had his partner's body across his shoulders and was jogging for the fire stairs at the back of the atrium.

"Stop!"

The word was weak on his lips, but it carried well enough. Ash paused at the stairwell's door, a victor's grin on his face as he stared back at him. Carter climbed to his feet as the merc pulled a silver zippo lighter from his pocket, flicked the flint-wheel and tossed it back into the room. It hit a kerosene soaked rug and within a heartbeat, flame was spreading across the floor towards the pile of furniture. Ash gave him a mock salute across the burning room, then passed into the stairwell and slammed the door as the hotel's fire alarm began to wail.

Black smoke billowed up to the ceiling high above, the acrid stink making Carter's eyes water. Behind him in the bar, Soul Feeders shrieked with fury. The floor trembled as a stack of furniture crashed to the ground—they had broken past the obstruction of their own dead.

It was enough to fire his adrenaline. Carter had to move or he was going to be caught between a choice of two deaths, neither of which appealed. The doors separating the bar from the atrium were wood, carved with intricate designs of leaves and animals. Caring little for the hours of labour that must have gone into the artistic representation of nature, Carter was just glad the doors were bloody heavy and thick. He slammed them closed and jammed the legs of a chair over the top of the handles to hold them fast.

As the chair legs dropped into place, the door trembled as a beast crashed into the far side. The aluminium legs of the chair flexed, but held for the moment. Carter looked at the clear strip on the side of his magazine, counting less than a dozen rounds at his disposal. He needed to move. Gritting his teeth against the pain of his chest, he skirted the wall of the room, staying clear of the blaze in the centre. The furniture was well alight, flame rapidly crawling across the wooden floor, spreading outward in a growing molten pool.

As he reached the fire stairs at the far end of the atrium, the door to the bar smashed open. Five Soul Feeders spilled through the gap, saliva frothing at their jaws. They skidded to a stop before the flames, wary of the blistering heat. Instead of venturing farther into the room, they began to retreat, turning for the bar again.

Fuck. As much as he hated putting himself on the hook, they needed bait or the plan was dead.

"Hey, you spiky-handed motherfuckers!" screamed Carter. The huge insects spun around at his voice, eyes locking onto him across the inferno. "That's right, I killed your shitty brothers. Come and get me!"

The Soul Feeders screamed, dropped to all fours and launched at him, followed by more from the bar. Carter grabbed the door handle to enter the emergency stairwell, but it didn't budge. The damn thing was locked.

You've got to be fucking kidding me.

Carter glanced at the elevator, but the outside buttons were already flashing 'out of order' due to the fire alarm. He lifted his rifle and shot the two leading beasts, their carcasses rolling into the fire as their kindred scurried past.

Carter looked around for a way out and latched onto the closest thing at hand. A long narrow banner hung from the mezzanine area high above. Allowing his rifle to hang from its sling, he took a fistful of the fabric and began to climb. Made from some sort of nylon composite, the material was slippery but strong. Arm after arm he pulled himself higher, focusing only on the next hold. Busted ribs creaked and burned like acid with every breath and change in grip, but it was a pain that was bearable if it meant he was escaping the beasts below.

Suddenly, the banner shook violently. Carter's legs slipped free, leaving him hanging from one hand. The banner slid through his grip, dropping an arm-span before Carter managed to gain hold with both hands again. He looked down, saw a swarm of Soul Feeders below. One crouched and leapt upwards, bayonet-like claw extended. Carter brought his feet up onto the wall and kicked himself to the side, swinging on the banner in an arc. The beast missed, claw punching clear air where his buttocks had been a split second earlier. He wound the banner around his left hand, then used his right to grab the rifle from where it hung on its sling. Flicking to auto, he sprayed two short bursts of gunfire at the beasts below, shredding the arms of the beast holding the fabric. The magazine ran dry all too quickly and he unclipped the sling, discarding the now useless weapon as unneeded weight, and gripped back onto the banner with both hands.

Carter kept climbing, ignoring the pain in his chest, focusing only on the mezzanine level above. One last effort, and he finally rolled over the handrail and onto the floor. Chest heaving to catch his breath, Carter forced himself to stand. He wiped spit from the corner of his mouth and the fingers came away red. Carter growled in frustration; a punctured lung was the last thing he needed. He peered down over the mezzanine's handrail and saw the last Soul Feeder sprint past the fire to join his brothers at the base of the wall.

Carter looked back deeper into the room and gave a hawkish grin. The growing fire had finally reached either side of the room, closing off the beasts' escape route with a wall of flame. Choking, black smoke was thick in the air, forcing Carter to pull the top of his shirt up over his mouth as a substandard filter.

Down below, the insects writhed in a panicked mess as they realised they were trapped. Some unfurled their tiny wings, but the tissue was too frail for the enormous heat. As they crossed over the bonfire, the wings caught flame, curling away in an instant to send them falling directly into the blaze. Others tried to sprint through the flame, creating a pathway of fallen corpses at the margins of the room, but none passed more than halfway across the atrium before their exoskeletons cracked in the furnace and caught fire. High-pitched squeals of agony sounded in tandem to the blaring fire alarm, the death throes of a hidden species.

Amber flames streaked up the banner he'd climbed, turning it to a melting ooze of blue goop. Carter coughed into his shirt and backed away from the edge, one hand up to shield his face from the heat. In the absence of the disabled sprinklers, the fire was rapidly spreading out of control. Carter jogged to the fire stairwell, and breathed a sigh of relief as the door opened.

Carter stepped into the stairwell and slammed the door shut behind. Compared to the landing outside, the stairs were an oasis of clean air and coolness. Staring upward, he grimaced. He knew Ash had placed a seed of doubt about Rylan for a reason. Concern at Rylan's ability to regenerate was legitimate, but instinct screamed the merc was not to be trusted. His partner had said something earlier about Silver-Trust, something niggling at the back of his mind.

You friggin' dumb ass.

Silver-Trust were researching senolytics, searching for the fountain of youth and a cure to aging. Rylan had said they wanted the Soul Feeders to study for the longevity. They'd been incorrect in that assumption of long life, but now Freidman had a new candidate to study. No wonder the billionaire had sent his attack dog after her! Rylan was the Holy Grail to their research, a creature that could heal from catastrophic wounds and was immune to the standard processes of aging. If anyone would stoop to selling her physiological secrets to Australia's enemies, it was Freidman. The man had the conscience of a pit-viper.

Ash had a large head start on him for the roof. But even for an athlete, climbing ten storeys with a full grown adult across your shoulders represented a test of endurance. He could only hope there was still time to catch them before they reached the helicopter. Carter grit his teeth and started running.

CHAPTER SEVENTEEN

Her body slung roughly across Ash's shoulders, Rylan gasped as she reanimated. Pain burnt through her chest like a hot poker, tissue damaged by the bullet's path screaming at every movement. The bodyguard was jogging up the stairs, breathing heavy, grunting under her weight. Each step tortured her body, his shoulder gouging at the partially healed gunshot wound in her upper chest. Rylan knew she needed to make a move, but for the moment, she barely had the strength to breathe, let along fight. Ash turned the corner on a landing, uncaring as her head crashed into the concrete wall. A cry of pain escaped her lips before she could clamp them shut.

The bodyguard skidded to a halt and dumped her on the ground like a sack of grain. She yelped as a vertebra snapped on the corner of a step, sending a shock of electric pain down her left leg.

"You're back then, eh?" he said, drawing a handgun from inside his jacket. "We've got another few flights to go, and I don't need you fighting back. See you top side, darlin'."

The merc aimed the gun at her head. Rylan stared into the muzzle's black eye of death, fury mounting as he pulled the trigger.

***

Carter flinched at the gunshot, then leaned over the handrail and looked up. He saw the briefest movement in the gloom maybe five flights above— closer than expected.

Carter held his breath, straining for any sound from Rylan.

Nothing. Just the sound of heavy footsteps taking off again. Carter ejected his pistol's magazine and counted one shot remaining. It would have to fly true, or he'd be fighting with nothing more than a knife, fists and a heart filled with rage. Gun tight in his grip, Carter grit his teeth and set off in pursuit.

***

"Wakey, wakey. Time to get moving, love."

Rylan opened her left eye, but struggled to focus on the leering Englishman bent over her. Her right eye still wasn't working, the lids fused together while the globe regenerated beneath. Blood-stained tears oozed from its corner in a line down Rylan's cheek. Her chest still ached, but it was nothing compared to her head. The bullet had mashed a path through eye and brain, exiting in a spray of blood and bone. Brain injuries always hurt the most, leaving her with debilitating migraines for weeks afterward.

They were on the hotel roof beside the fire stairs, on a small square of level concrete. The helipad was thirty metres away, accessible by a narrow metal bridge with waist high hand rails of twisted steel wire. Half of the space by the stairwell was taken up with firefighting equipment. Potential fuel leaks or engine problems during approach mandated the presence of fire-fighting equipment on landing. In a metal cupboard with a clear plexiglass door, stood a foam extinguisher, jaws of life and fireman's axe.

"Three," said Rylan, her voice thick as she tried to sit up.

"Huh?"

"Three fucking times you've killed me now," she growled. Rylan slipped a hand under her shirt, fingering the lumpy scar of a closed bullet wound as she noted the axe. "Before there were planes, I once crossed oceans to get revenge on someone that killed me *just once*. There's nowhere on Earth you'll be safe from me. That's a promise."

Ash just laughed. "You're welcome to try, but people have been trying to kill me for the last twenty years, and I'm still here."

A thunder of helicopter blades buffeted her eardrums as Freidman's craft passed overhead. It hovered above the landing pad at the end of the walkway for a moment before slowly descending, twin skids clumping onto the circle of concrete with a slight bounce before settling. Jet black, it was an ACH130 with enclosed tail rotor. Able to carry up to six passengers, the back door slid open to reveal the billionaire. Freidman appeared agitated, yelling something to Ash, but the rotor wash drowned out his voice.

Ash grabbed her by the shoulder and forced her to stand. "On your feet. It's time to go."

Rylan used the added momentum to lunge past him, but her injured brain fumbled the commands to her legs. She tripped over her own feet, smashing heavily into her target—the fire cupboard. Rylan ripped the plexiglass door open, and almost had the axe in hand before Ash kicked her arm aside.

"Come on, Agent. Don't you know when you're beaten?"

A crack of gunfire sounded from the helicopter. Both of them looked back, and saw the old billionaire pointing a handgun at the roof below. It bucked in his hands twice more, the muzzle flash bright orange in the dark.

"What the fuck?" said Ash.

He slammed the cupboard door shut and peered over the top of it, looking in the direction of Freidman's fire. A spike of obsidian claw stabbed into the top of the cabinet, missing his face by a hair. Ash staggered backward as a large Soul Feeder pulled itself up over the rail and onto the platform.

Rylan realised it must have climbed the side of the building. If the swarm had avoided the blaze, it could be the first of many. The beast screamed, pincers spread wide as it lunged for the merc. Ash raised his rifle and shot from the hip, a burst of rounds on full automatic that emptied his magazine and decimated the creature's waist. The Soul Feeder's legs collapsed, but it was far from dead. It crawled forward, dragging its limp lower body with powerful arms. Reversing the weapon, Ash slammed the rifle's stock into the beast's face, cracking the right pincer. The Soul Feeder punched the merc's leg, dagger-like talon extended. The long claw skewered his thigh from side to side like a bayonet. Ash cried out in agony, teeth bared as he grasped the remaining pincer with both hands, desperate to keep its venomous tip from his flesh.

Rylan flung open the cupboard and ripped the axe from its housing. Using it as a crutch, she heaved herself to standing. One more poke from the beast's claw and she would lose her chance for revenge. Rylan still couldn't quite feel the fingers on her left hand, the grip clumsy as she hoisted the axe overhead. Rylan swung the blade down with all her strength, grunting as the movement spiked agony through her skull.

The heavy blade cut through the exoskeleton of the beast's head with a wet crunch, spraying blood and brains in the merc's face. The creature hit the deck hard, dragging Ash to the concrete by his thigh. He snarled, teeth red with his own blood as he heaved the talon back through his leg.

Rylan levered at the axe blade. Her strength was returning as healing progressed, but not fast enough. She planted a boot on the back of the Soul Feeder's head, finally extracting her weapon with another savage tug. A harsh grin lit Rylan's face like a Valkyrie. The axe felt good in her hands as the last of the numbness ebbed away. On battlefields past, it had always been her weapon of choice, one fitting for revenge.

Holding her eye, Ash's hand went to his waist, appearing again with a combat knife in his grip. In a fluid movement, it left his hand, thrown in a blur of silver for her neck. Rylan batted the knife away with the axe's haft, then swung her weapon overhead to finish the job.

Something smashed into her chest with the force of a sledge-hammer as a gunshot sounded from the chopper, knocking her aim off centre. Ash screamed as the axe cut into his left forearm, severing the limb at the wrist. Rylan staggered backward, losing hold of the axe as she coughed blood in a spray of carmine droplets. Over on the helipad, Freidman stood at the far side of the walkway with gun in hand. He strode across, face red with fury as he knelt beside his bodyguard and wound a belt about the merc's wrist until the severed arteries stopped squiring blood.

"For fucks sake. Do I have to do everything myself around here?" he growled.

Rylan sat down hard, her chest burning with every breath. She concentrated on staying conscious. If the bullet had missed any major vasculature and passed front to back through a lung, she'd be back in the fight in a minute or two.

Freidman glared at her as he walked to a control panel next to the fire equipment and entered a code to turn on the sprinklers in the main building. "You are proving a little more work than I expected, Agent, and maybe too much for me to get out of the country without a little more preparation." He glanced at his bodyguard for a moment before turning back to her with a glint of amusement in his eye. "But then again, maybe I need to think outside the box. Your healing powers are quite extraordinary; have you ever had part of your body amputated? I wonder if it is possible for you to heal from the other side?"

He turned to Ash. "If we confiscated a leg, it'd surely take a few days to grow a body? Give us time to leave the country without drama?"

Ash heaved himself to his feet, jaw clenched against the pain. He leaned down and picked up the axe, studying the bloodied metal for a second before looking at her.

"I reckon you're onto something, boss. But if we're taking limbs, I'd rather finish the trade properly. She took my hand, I think it's only right I get hers."

Freidman barked a harsh laugh and slapped his bodyguard on the back. "Have it your way, but hurry up. We need to get moving." He turned on his heel and jogged back across the walkway to the chopper.

"Okay, love, keep still now. Wouldn't want to take any more than necessary, eh?"

Rylan screamed as the blade passed through the bones of her wrist, sparks flying as the axe bit into the concrete below.

CHAPTER EIGHTEEN

Carter bounded up the last flight of stairs, each breath rasping like a file against his broken ribs. Spurred on by the Soul Feeder's metallic screams, adrenaline powered his last burst of speed. Desperation to join the fight and protect his partner brushed aside any thoughts of his own safety. As he neared the door, a fresh scream cut the air.

Rylan!

He slammed into the door, shoulder smashing it aside to re-enter the night. Rylan lay to the side of the stairwell cradling her wrist, while Ash and Freidman thundered over the metal walkway, escaping to the helipad. The bodyguard dragged his left leg, blood oozing from a ragged thigh wound. The chopper's engine whined as the blades twirled into life, quickly becoming a blur of metal.

"You okay?" he asked Rylan. A blood-spattered chin, along with an oozing bullet wound to her right upper chest gave him the answer. She was a mess, one eye seeping red tears between swollen lids.

"You need to stop them," she grunted. "They have my hand."

Carter's gut clenched as she lifted a ragged stump. Spurting arteries slowed to a trickle before his eyes as Rylan's body minimised blood loss and began to heal.

"It's all Freidman needs to begin his research."

He couldn't allow that to happen. Carter lifted his handgun and stared over the sights, tracking the merc as he neared the end of the walkway. Just as he squeezed the trigger, Ash stumbled, Carter's shot buzzing past like an angry hornet an inch over his head.

Carter swore viciously. "That was my last round."

Ash glanced back over his shoulder, eyes widening as he spotted Carter for the first time. "Give me your gun!" he shouted to his boss. Freidman leaned out the chopper's door and passed his pistol to the merc, taking Rylan's hand in exchange.

Carter clenched his jaw, knowing he was down to a knife. Not a way to enter a gunfight if you wanted to live.

"Use me as a body shield," coughed Rylan. "I'll heal again, you won't. There's no choice."

Carter didn't question it, knowing his partner was right.

"Give me the axe, and don't let me drop."

Carter pulled Rylan to her feet then stood behind, holding a fistful of her jacket in one hand, her belt with the other.

"Go!" shouted Rylan.

Carter drove onward, Rylan taking most of her own weight. The first bullet hit before they'd even reached the bridge to the helipad, rocking her shoulder back. She growled, but maintained her feet. The next two shots hit her gut, bursting through the small of her back to bury in Carter's bulletproof vest. She sagged in his grip, much of the strength going from her legs.

Ash was less than five paces away. For the first time, his confident mask began to slip. Behind him, the helicopter's skids began to lift. Ash backed away, his last shot going wide as he finally turned to run.

"He's mine!" growled Rylan as they closed.

She grunted, a last effort of strength to swing the axe one handed, burying the blade deep in the bodyguard's neck.

Carter released his grip on Rylan, drew his knife and sprinted the last three steps to the chopper. Air blasted down at him from the spinning blades as he dove for the closing doorway. He caught hold of a seat belt with his left hand, his legs dangling until they found the skid. Freidman scooted back, holding Rylan's severed hand to his chest like a child with a bloody talisman as Carter struggled to maintain his footing.

"Give me the hand, Freidman!" Carter risked a glance down, and saw the ground would soon be outside jumping distance. He grit his teeth and lunged forward, stabbing his knife into the leather between the billionaire's legs.

"Last chance; the next one'll take your balls."

Freidman recoiled and flicked the limp hand at him. Carter let go of his knife, catching the hand mid-air and jumped backwards. For a second there was nothing but rushing wind, and then a crunch as he hit the helipad. His ankle twisted as he thumped onto the tarmac, winded. Carter lay on his back, mouth gaping until he finally caught his breath. Above, the helicopter lifted quickly, soon disappearing over a ridgeline to the south and into the night.

Finally, Carter willed himself back onto his feet. He hadn't felt this bad since waking in an Afghan field hospital, peppered with shrapnel. Everything hurt, but his minor wounds paled to insignificance when he thought of his partner. Snow fell gently as he limped slowly over to Rylan and Ash's bodies. As he neared, Rylan opened her eyes. She looked exhausted, a tiredness that spoke of centuries of pain and toil.

"Did you get it?"

Carter nodded and stared down at the amputated limb in his hand. Instead of torn, bloodied tissue at the wrist, skin had already grown across the stump. He passed it to her, before staring at their foe. Ash was face down and silent, a pool of dark blood spreading beneath his torso and head. Carter gripped the axe haft, levered the blade from the corpse's neck and placed it on the ground. After what the man had done to Rylan, he didn't begrudge her revenge, even if it left his gut a little on edge that the man had been running away when the fatal blow landed.

Carter sighed, and eased himself to the tarmac opposite his partner. He noticed the cold for the first time in hours, and shivered as it wormed down the back of his neck with icy fingers. Freidman's state of the art sprinkler system and fire compartments through the hotel seemed to have done their job in stopping the spread of the blaze. White smoke of an extinguished fire sifted up from the far side of the building, and there was no sign of flames elsewhere in the complex.

He cocked his head to the side, listening. Aside from the tinnitus whine of his damaged eardrums, there was nothing but the gentle rustle of a breeze through the surrounding bush. It was over.

CHAPTER NINETEEN

An earth-mover's metal tracks rumbled away, leaving the mass-grave ready for concealment. Soldiers moved in with rolls of turf to cover the bare soil. By the time they were finished, the burial site would be indistinguishable from other newly landscaped areas about the hotel.

"I wish these bastards could have been here yesterday," muttered Carter. Surviving on caffeine and pain killers, he was buggered.

The special-ops soldiers had arrived early that morning to aid Carter and Rylan in the clean-up operation, removing all evidence of the beasts from the mountain. Aside from three carcasses retained for research purposes, the rest had been incinerated on site, their ashes now buried deep in the earth.

Carter's head turned toward the hotel's train platform as a carriage pulled up. A small medical team piled out with bags in hand. Obviously keen to be on their way home, the group headed straight for their van. All except an older man with wire rimmed glasses who departed the group, angling toward Rylan.

"The staff and guests located at the evacuation point have been sanitized. Before we leave, I wanted to re-confirm that no other people came in contact with the cryptids?"

Rylan frowned. "Just Freidman, the Silver-Trust CEO. But he's probably already skipped the country."

The doctor grimaced. "Unfortunate. That may present problems in the future." Without another word, he abruptly turned on the spot and strode back to his colleagues. He climbed into the back and slid the door shut, the van pulling onto the road moments later.

The medical group had administered a dose of Oblivizide to civilian witnesses. Developed specifically for black-ops, the medication caused retrograde amnesia while inducing high susceptibility to suggestion. Nobody would recall contact with the Soul Feeders. Instead, they left with a story for the media on their lips, of a horrific fire that had tragically stolen the lives of numerous guests.

Carter looked down at the metal waste paper bin in his hand. "Where do you want to do this?"

She shrugged. "Here will do."

He dumped the bin on the snow, then poured in a large splash of petrol as Rylan tossed in an object wrapped in brown paper.

Carter lit a match and held it at the rim. "Ready?"

She nodded and he dropped the flame. The accelerant ignited, burning through the paper to reveal Rylan's amputated hand. Half the forearm had already grown back. Hairs rose on the back of Carter's neck as the fingers started to twitch, scrabbling at the sides of the bin as the hand sought to escape the inferno. The skin blistered and blackened, fat melting away to expose red muscle. Tissue charred, emitting an awful stench of burnt pork mixed with petrol. The limb eventually fell still.

"Would it have kept on growing?" asked Carter, a sour taste in the back of his throat.

"You mean, would it have created my clone?" said Rylan. "With the way it was going, probably a good chance. Creeps me out a little to tell the truth."

Carter raised an eyebrow in question, waiting for her to continue.

"I've been injured in a similar way a few times in the past, but never had the opportunity to see what happened to the limb. Makes me a little uneasy to think I might have a second body running around somewhere."

Rylan glanced down at her healing limb. Overnight, the wrist and palm had grown from the stump. Little nubs of white protruded from the end of the palm, the early beginnings of fingers. She winced, then raised the healing limb and wiped at her right eye.

"How's it feeling?" asked Carter. "Have you got sight back yet?"

"Yeah, it's okay, just tearing a little."

Her sight might be back, but Carter doubted all was fine, not with the way she kept rubbing at it. For the first time, the damaged tissue hadn't repaired perfectly. In stark contrast to the left side, the iris of the healed eye was now blood-red.

Rylan glanced up at a noise, then shoved her stump deep into a jacket pocket, her face hardening as one of the special-ops soldiers ran toward her with a satellite phone. Carter stood in front of the bin, blocking the soldier's view of their macabre barbeque.

"Agent Rylan?" he asked. "I have ASIO Director Tiller on the phone."

She gave a tight nod and took the phone. Carter watched Rylan's face as she listened intently to the Director before handing the phone back to the soldier. As the Corporal retreated, her mouth twisted like she wanted to spit.

Carter had seen that sort of expression on previous officers before. It was the sort of face that said leave was cancelled for the foreseeable future. "Out with it. Where's the next case?"

Rylan turned, and met his gaze. "Northern Territory. Something big has taken out a whole tour group in the wetlands of Kakadu."

"Saltwater crocodile?"

"Maybe, but last I heard, they didn't grow to forty feet." She turned and started for the hotel car park. "Either way, we'll find out soon enough. The Director's organised a plane to meet us at Mt. Hotham Airport; we fly out in two hours."

Carter stared into the bin where Rylan's hand was now nothing more than blackened bone and ash. A carnivorous forty-foot monster?

Well that's just fucking fantastic.

A few days earlier he would have scoffed at the possibility, but not anymore. Carter took a deep breath, one arm splinting his ribs before following after his boss. At least there was one bonus. With any luck, at least he'd get some sleep on the flight.

THE END

@severec
/severedpress

Check out other great

Cryptid Novels!

J.H. Moncrieff

RETURN TO DYATLOV PASS

In 1959, nine Russian students set off on a skiing expedition in the Ural Mountains. Their mutilated bodies were discovered weeks later. Their bizarre and unexplained deaths are one of the most enduring true mysteries of our time. Nearly sixty years later, podcast host Nat McPherson ventures into the same mountains with her team, determined to finally solve the mystery of the Dyatlov Pass incident. Her plans are thwarted on the first night, when two trackers from her group are brutally slaughtered. The team's guide, a superstitious man from a neighboring village, blames the killings on yetis, but no one believes him. As members of Nat's team die one by one, she must figure out if there's a murderer in their midst—or something even worse—before history repeats itself and her group becomes another casualty of the infamous Dead Mountain.

Gerry Griffiths

CRYPTID ZOO

As a child, rare and unusual animals, especially cryptid creatures, always fascinated Carter Wilde. Now that he's an eccentric billionaire and runs the largest conglomerate of high-tech companies all over the world, he can finally achieve his wildest dream of building the most incredible theme park ever conceived on the planet... CRYPTID ZOO. Even though there have been apparent problems with the project, Wilde still decides to send some of his marketing employees and their families on a forced vacation to assess the theme park in preparation for Opening Day. Nick Wells and his family are some of those chosen and are about to embark on what will become the most terror-filled weekend of their lives—praying they survive. STEP RIGHT UP AND GET YOUR FREE PASS... TO CRYPTID ZOO

Printed in Great Britain
by Amazon